MOON FATED

SHADOW PACK LEGENDS #1

LUNA M. ROSE

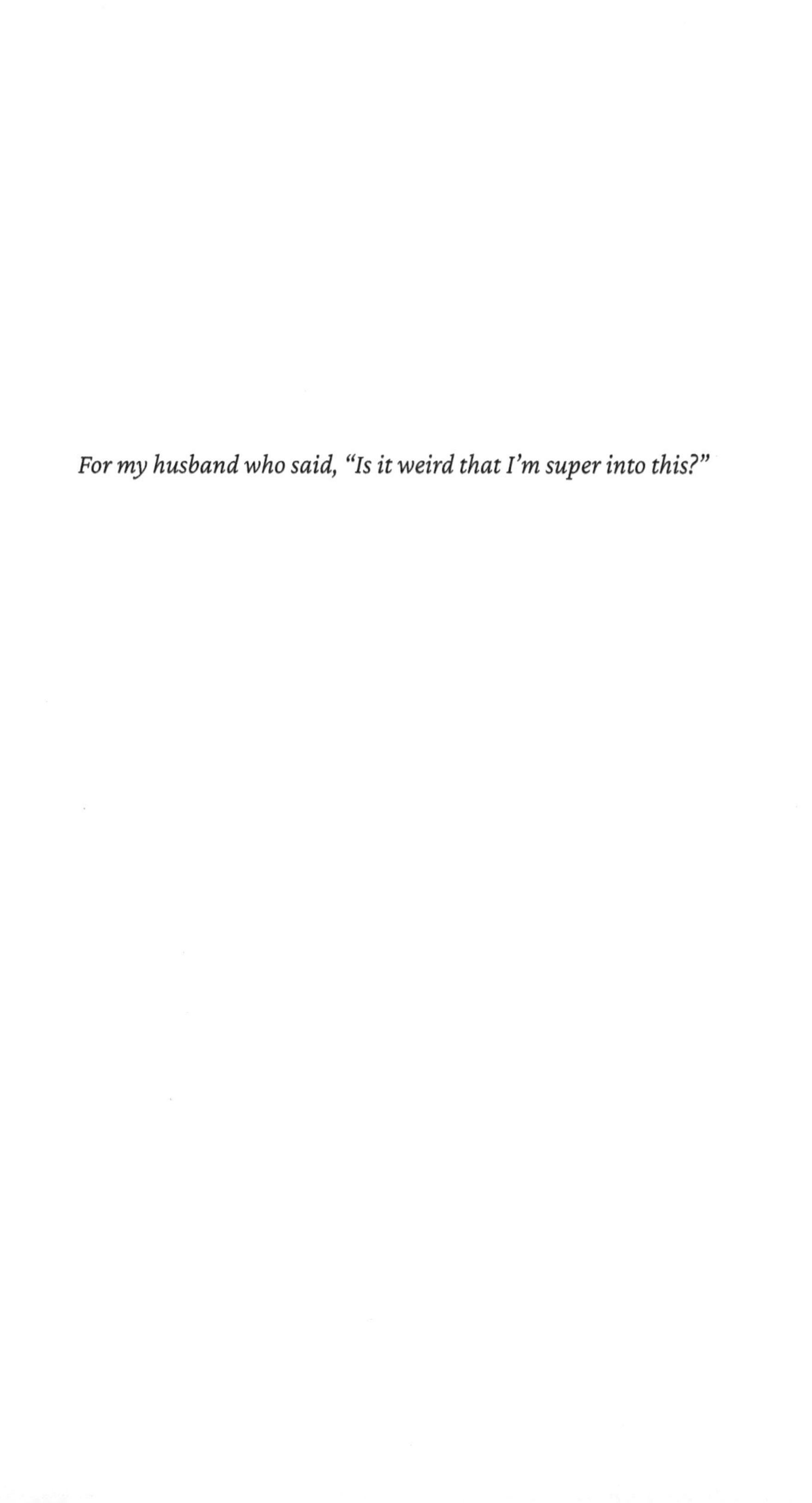

For my husband who said, "Is it weird that I'm super into this?"

CHAPTER
ONE

EVELYN

S irens wailed behind me as I wove through the crowded Seattle streets, my heart pounding in rhythm with my hurried footsteps. The chaos of the city clamored for my attention—honking cars, chattering pedestrians, the distant echo of construction work—but I barely registered any of it, my mind solely fixated on the intersection of Cambert and Pine St.

Dispatch had called in a Code Blue moments ago, and every second counted. I'd learned to navigate the pandemonium of emergencies, but the urgency never diminished. A life hung in the balance, and my duty was to ensure they had a fighting chance.

I pushed past a group of tourists, their cameras flashing in my peripheral vision. A few disgruntled shouts floated after me, and I wanted to flip them the bird. The arrogance of some people. Crowding around one of their own as if their suffering was a circus act presented for their entertainment.

But thoughts like that made me angry, and I couldn't afford to let any strong emotion take hold. For more reasons than one. It wasn't safe to react emotionally in the field, and it wasn't safe for me personally.

The tense knot in my stomach tightened with each step, adrenaline and anxiety mixing in my stomach like rocket fuel.

Two more blocks.

I rounded the corner, my hand instinctively reaching for the radio at my hip. "ETA 90 seconds." My voice strained against the burning in my lungs. Static crackled in response, followed by an acknowledgment from my partner, Bruce. His real name was Jack, but he was an asshole so I took the liberty of giving him the name his mother should have.

The scene came into view, a small crowd gathered around a prone form on the sidewalk. I quickened my pace, my training kicking into high gear as I mentally ran through the protocols.

Check for responsiveness. Assess airway, breathing, circulation. Begin resuscitation if necessary.

I shouldered my way through the onlookers, my focus narrowing to the lifeless body before me. The world faded away, replaced by the singular goal of saving the person at my feet.

I dropped to my knees beside the unconscious man, my hands already moving to check his vital signs. If the pockmarks on his cheeks and bleeding gums weren't enough of an indicator, his skin was pale and clammy, his breathing shallow and erratic.

Overdose.

"Sir, can you hear me?" My words were steady despite the

hammering of my heart. No response. I turned to the nearest bystander, a middle-aged woman with fear etched on her face. "Did anyone see what happened?"

She nodded, her eyes wide. "He just collapsed. I think... I think he was on something?"

I acknowledged her with a brief nod, my attention already back on my patient. His pulse was weak and thready beneath my fingertips, a stark contrast to the adrenaline surging through my veins.

"I need space," I barked, my voice cutting through the crowd's murmurs. They stepped back, giving me room to work. I reached for my bag, my hands moving with practiced precision as I retrieved the necessary equipment. Naloxone. A syringe. An airway adjunct. Bruce, as usual, puffed out his chest and postured as if he planned to save a life through sheer douchery.

It was easiest to ignore him in moments like these. When the world narrowed to this moment, this life in my hands. I drew up the naloxone, my movements swift and sure. There was no room for hesitation, no time for second-guessing.

I positioned the syringe, finding the vein, then drew a deep breath and exhaled as I pressed. The needle slipped beneath his skin, and I pushed the plunger, watching as the life-saving medication disappeared into his bloodstream.

Come on, fight, I willed. Seconds ticked by, each one an eternity. I monitored his vital signs, ready to begin CPR if needed. The crowd around me held its collective breath.

And then, a gasp. A flicker of movement beneath his eyelids. The man's chest heaved as he drew in a ragged breath, color slowly returning to his face. Relief washed over me, tempered by the knowledge that the battle was far from over. But for now, I'd given him a chance.

I leaned in close, my voice gentle but firm. "Hey, can you hear me? You're going to be okay. We're EMT's and we're here to help you."

The man's eyes fluttered open, hazy and unfocused. He tried to speak, but his words came out as a hoarse whisper.

"Don't try to talk just yet," I soothed, placing a reassuring hand on his shoulder. "We're going to take good care of you. You're safe now."

I could see the fear in his eyes, the unspoken questions. How close had he come to the edge? What would have happened if we hadn't arrived in time? *Had he wanted us to arrive in time?*

"You're stronger than you know." I held his gaze. "You fought hard today, and you won. This is a new beginning, a chance to start over."

Every time I gave that speech I remembered when I'd given it to myself. Three years ago. When I packed a duffel and drove to Seattle.

I couldn't help but feel a twinge of empathy for the man lying before me as my team—not Bruce, who was busy consoling a woman on the edge of the crowd wearing a tank top that cut to her belly button—worked around me, attaching monitors and starting an IV.

I knew all too well the darkness that could drive someone to such desperate measures. The scars on my own soul were a testament to the battles I hadn't fought. The bully I tore myself away from. Maybe I couldn't go back and kick the hell out of Nathan Black, but I could show up night after night and fight for people who couldn't fight for themselves.

Something nobody did for me when I needed it most.

∼

Exhaustion hit me like a freight train as I stumbled into my apartment, the weight of the day heavy on my shoulders. The silence that greeted me was a stark contrast to the chaos of blaring sirens and shouting voices still echoing in my mind.

I leaned against the door, closing my eyes momentarily as I settled my breathing. The solitude was both a comfort and a curse, a reminder of the emptiness that trailed me like a lost puppy. I wanted this. *I chose this.*

With a heavy sigh, I pushed off the door and went to the kitchen, my feet dragging with each step. I grabbed a glass from the cupboard and filled it with water.

When I first started renting this place, I'd planned to replace the 1970's curtains that hung like a pair of bloomers over the window above the sink. That was overly ambitious of me. As was the idea to purchase a new light fixture to replace the boob light over the kitchen table. That one had grown on me, though.

I sipped from the glass, the water cooling my parched throat, then jumped out of my skin as my phone vibrated on the counter. My cell, not my work phone that always sat in my back pocket.

Nobody ever called *my* phone.

I hesitated, a sense of unease washing over me. I had a feeling that whatever was waiting for me on that screen wouldn't be welcome news.

With a shaking hand, I reached for the phone. My heart pounded in my chest as I unlocked the screen. And there it was. A flood of missed calls and two text messages, all from the same person.

Blake Ash. My best friend's brother and the last person I expected to be reaching out to me. *Could I call her my best friend anymore?* I hadn't talked to her in over a year, but I certainly hadn't made any better relationships to take her place.

She was one of two people with this number, so if Blake was calling...

I scrolled through the messages, and my stomach dropped.

> Hey. It's Blake. Emergency. Call me.

> Evs, not joking. Call now pls

I took a deep breath, trying to steady my nerves as I hit the call button. The phone rang once, twice, before Blake's gruff voice answered. "Evelyn?"

"Blake, what's going on? Why are you calling on Callie's phone?" My words tumbled out in a rush.

There was a pause on the other end of the line, and I could hear the tension in Blake's voice when he finally spoke. "Callie's missing."

My heart stopped. For a moment, I forgot how to breathe. "What do you mean, missing?" I managed to choke out, my voice barely above a whisper.

"She didn't come home last night, and no one's seen her since yesterday afternoon." Blake's voice caught. "I've been trying to track her down, but obviously her phone is here."

I closed my eyes, trying to process the information. Callista was the most reliable person I knew, always checking in and letting someone know where she was going. For her to disappear like this? It was unthinkable.

"Do you have any idea where she might be?" It was a stupid question. If he had her phone and had resorted to calling me, he'd likely exhausted his other options. *Why had she left her phone?* My mind raced with possibilities, none of them good given my profession.

Blake sighed heavily. "No, nothing. That's why I'm calling you. I thought maybe she might have said something to you, given how close you two are. Were."

Ouch. That stung. I shook my head, even though he couldn't see me. "No, I haven't heard from her."

The silence stretched between us, heavy with unspoken fears. Finally, Blake spoke again. "I don't know what to do. I've never seen anything like this before. It's like she just vanished into thin air. And with the others—"

"What others?"

"You don't know?"

"How would I know, Blake?" I snapped, then pursed my lips. "I'm sorry. No. I haven't talked to anyone from Kitimat since last September." That was the last time Callista and I talked.

"She's not the first." I could hear the desperation in his voice, and it mirrored the growing sense of dread in my own stomach.

"What are you saying? There are more members of our pack who have gone missing?"

The phone scraped against his cheek. "Merrill. Beth."

Air hissed through my teeth. "What the hell? Since when?"

"Merrill left back in May. I didn't think much of it. He wasn't—you know what I mean."

Yeah. I did. Merrill had always been a little off.

Blake exhaled. "But Callie wouldn't do something like this. Neither would Beth."

"We'll find her, Blake." I tried to sound more confident than I felt. What was I saying? We? There was no we, not anymore. I'd told Callie as much last time we'd talked. But this was in my skill set. How could I sit here and not try?

As if reading my thoughts, Blake cleared his throat. "Nathan's up north."

"For how long?"

"Not sure. A week, maybe? We're not the only pack having trouble."

I stared at the cream backsplash behind the faucet, forgetting to blink until my eyes burned.

"Will you come back?" Blake asked. He already knew the answer. When I didn't reply, he said, "We don't know what we're dealing with yet. Be careful."

"I will," I promised, still holding the phone to my ear after the line went dead.

Callista was missing. *Callista was missing.* She was my rock, the one person who had always been there for me, no matter what. The thought of something happening to her was too much to bear. I had to do something, had to find a way to help. I owed Callista that much and more.

As I dropped my arm and strode out of the kitchen, the weariness from my long shift vanished, replaced by a fierce, unwavering resolve. I moved through my apartment with purpose, gathering supplies.

I packed a duffel bag with a few changes of clothes, a flashlight, snacks, and all of the cash I'd stuffed into the back of my underwear drawer. Questions swirled in my head but there was one that kept drifting to the surface. *Had Nathan hurt her too?*

Guilt swirled through me like a drink mix in a water bottle. If I hadn't left, maybe Callie would still be there. If I'd spoken up. If I'd gone to the council. If I'd been the loyal beta. If I hadn't abandoned my pack. *If. If. If.*

Not helpful. Anger and grief simmered until I could feel my wolf under the surface again, gnawing to break free. *No.* I drew on my crisis training, honing in on the task immediately in front of me as I forced air into my lungs.

Slamming my toiletries into the bag, I zipped it shut and hoisted it over my shoulder, then surveyed the room for anything I might've missed.

Nathan's up north.

A week. I had one week, possibly less, to find what I could and disappear again. I loved Callie, but I would not allow my alpha to look me in the eyes again.

With a deep breath, I stepped out into the hallway, closing the door with a definitive click. The hunt was on.

ROWAN

My office didn't look like much at the end of the day. Reports strewn across my desk, part orders and receipts stacked in their respective baskets. I needed to go digital and get rid of the endless paper trail, but with the pack's rising needs in prior months, I hadn't been able to scrape away minutes for myself let alone a records overhaul.

The room hummed with the air filter, the soft tick of the wall clock the only other sound echoing through the space. I rose from my desk, rolling my shoulders to ease the tension that had settled there like a stubborn squatter. My muscles protested, a reminder of the physical toll my human form endured while shouldering the responsibilities of an alpha.

"Finished," I murmured to the empty room, and even spoken to myself, the words felt like a lie. Nothing had truly felt finished since Nathan's betrayal, since the day he turned his back on us and tore this pack apart at the seams.

Once a guardian who stood by my side, once a brother-in-arms, he'd ripped away the trust that had bonded us. Even five years later, his name was like a snarl on my tongue, a growl trapped within the confines of my chest that yearned to be unleashed.

He had been one of us, part of the Black Lake Pack, until his ambition poisoned him. Until he became a traitor not just to me but to all we had sworn to protect. I hated that our current circumstances dredged all the memories to the surface.

I forced those thoughts aside for now. There would be time for retribution, time for letting the wolf inside roam free and seek justice. But not yet.

Not yet. It was always not yet. Duty called with an iron voice, and as alpha, I couldn't afford to ignore it. I had to rebuild. I had to protect.

I wasn't like Nathan, ruling with an iron fist in his pack from the horror stories I'd heard. I had control in some circumstances, but in most, my pack members were free to live their lives. We took care of each other, and I hoped they could look to me in their time of need.

Now, there was talk of an all-pack meeting to deal with these mysterious disappearances, and I didn't know what the right move was. It's not that I didn't want to stand with the other rightful alpha's, but could I stand with him? Was it right to ask my pack to do so?

Yet I was still alpha of the Black Lake Pack. If anyone could restore what had been shattered, it was me. The thought was almost laughable. I'd been trying like hell, and where had it gotten me?

The door opened behind me with a soft click, and I found myself facing the narrowed eyes of my second. Jasper walked in and leaned against the wall, arms crossed over his broad chest. Beside him stood Lana, my third, her posture rigid as the redwoods guarding our territory, while Finn, the pack's healer, fiddled restlessly with the hem of his shirt. Their expressions were a mix of resolve and unease, mirroring the storm brewing within me.

"Let's skip the bullshit," Jasper's voice was rough. "You want to discuss the Kitimat Pack?"

Right to it, then.

"You want to help?" Lana's tone was sharp as flint. "After everything that's happened, you seriously think they deserve our aid?"

I walked past them, my boots thudding against the floorboards, and stopped at the window overlooking the dusky forest. The weight of leadership pressed on my shoulders, heavier than the mountains framing the horizon. "It's not about what they deserve," I started, but Finn cut in, his nostrils flaring.

"Rowan, they've never lifted a finger for us when we needed it. Why should we extend our protection now?"

I trusted Finn. His skepticism clawed at my resolve. They all had good reason for their doubts—trust was a luxury we could ill afford these days. But as alpha, it fell on me to see beyond our personal grievances.

"Jasper," I turned to face him squarely, holding his gaze. "Lana, Finn—we are not them." My words sliced through the room. "We are the Black Lake Pack. Our strength lies in unity, in the respect we hold for each other and for those outside our borders, no matter our history." It was the right thing to say. I knew it by the way their expressions shifted. I only wished I felt it in my heart.

Their faces softened as they wrestled with their loyalty and their frustration. It was a dance we knew all too well—one step forward, two steps back, always circling the fires of our shared purpose and individual fears.

"Helping the Kitimat Pack isn't only about them," I continued. "It's about us, who we are as a pack, as guardians of these lands."

Jasper's hands clenched into fists. When he spoke, his voice was a low rumble."Rowan, "Nathan Black—"

"Is not the whole of the Kitimat Pack," I cut in sharply, silencing the echoes of betrayal that his name conjured within the walls of our conclave. "They were once our brothers and sisters."

"Who sided with him," Lana muttered. Her intuition was as sharp as her fangs during a hunt, and her sense of justice sharper.

Finn, who had been quietly observing, finally spoke. "And if this is a trap? If helping them only leads to more danger?"

I clenched my jaw. "I don't think even he would make something like this up. You know the reports. It's not just Kitimat that's missing shifters."

Their eyes met mine, and in those piercing depths, I saw the reflection of my own determination. Gradually, the tension eased out of their broad shoulders. It was the subtle shift of pack mentality aligning behind their alpha—a silent affirmation of trust in my leadership.

I hoped it wasn't misplaced.

"So what, we agree to this pack meeting?" Jasper grimaced.

I nodded. "If it's called, we'll be there."

"I think they may come to us." Lana leaned against the back wall.

It made sense. The weather was already beginning to shift up north, and we still had a few months of passable roads ahead of us.

I ran a hand over my face. "I'll keep you informed."

Jasper clapped a hand on my shoulder. "You want to come out with us tonight? It's been a long week."

I thought about it. Just like I'd thought about it the last three times he'd asked. "I've got some loose ends I need to wrap up."

He paused, then nodded once. "Eat something. You look like shit."

I WENT TO THE BAR.

I knew I'd probably regret it. Not probably. Definitely. But the idea of stepping into my empty house alone with my warring thoughts made me antsy.

The dimly lit room buzzed with energy as I passed through the doorway, the familiar scents of whiskey and pine enveloping me. It wasn't hard to spot my pack in the back corner. It was always a variation of the same group, with Jasper and Lana as the steadies. Tonight, there were a few humans mixed in, which I loved to see. We'd been here in Black Lake long enough that the locals didn't blink at us anymore, but the rig pigs and wanderers moving in each summer were always a bit intimidated.

I chuckled to myself as I wove through the crowd. It wasn't surprising that we repelled mundanes. Lana in all black, her ink swirling out the side of her tank top on shoulders bigger than most of the men sitting at the bar. Jasper, with his grizzled beard and cap pulled low over his eyes.

It was good. If someone from town had the balls to approach, they'd be able to handle everything else beneath the rough exteriors.

The group erupted in boisterous cheers when they caught

sight of me. Jasper was at least three drinks deep. The Sully twins next to him were four by the look of their glassy eyes. It wouldn't last long with our metabolisms. "Rowan! Hell, man, about time you showed up!" Liam, my ever-loyal beta, clapped me on the back, his grin wide and infectious.

Before I could respond, I was swept up in a whirlwind of bear hugs and hearty handshakes, the pack's enthusiasm washing over me in waves. They dragged me toward the bar, pressing a cold beer into my hand and launching into animated chatter about their latest exploits. I loved hearing their stories, grateful not to talk about myself.

As the night wore on, the conversation inevitably turned to one of the topics I dreaded. There seemed to be too many to count these days.

"So, Rowan," Elijah, one of the younger wolves, leaned in conspiratorially, "when are you going to finally settle down with a mate?"

The others chimed in, their good-natured ribbing tinged with genuine concern. "Yeah, man. You can't be a lone wolf forever," Lucas chuckled, his eyes glinting with mischief.

I forced a smile. "You know how it is, guys. When fate decides it's time, I'll know."

The truth was, I'd always believed that my mate would be chosen by destiny, a deep, unbreakable bond forged by the moon goddess herself. That was how it had happened for my father and his brother. I wasn't naive enough to think I was entitled to a fated mate, but the goddess had chosen me as alpha. I'd shown up at the mating dances. I'd been open to it. But as the years passed and my packmates found their other halves, I couldn't help but feel a growing sense of disappointment and loneliness.

Mia, Liam's younger sister and ever the meddler, grinned

wickedly. "Well, if fate won't cooperate, maybe we should take matters into our own hands. Let's find Rowan a lady to take home tonight, eh?"

The pack erupted in laughter and cheers, but as they scanned the bar for potential candidates, I felt a sinking sensation in the pit of my stomach. This wasn't what I wanted, a meaningless fling with a human. I'd had plenty of those, and it only left me feeling more empty. I needed a partner. Someone who understood my responsibility and shouldered it with me. It was a big ask. Maybe too big.

"There." Mia pointed at a woman with long dark hair hanging down her back. She turned and smiled at her friend next to her. She had a pretty face, nice smile. I felt nothing, and Mia groaned as I shook my head.

As the laughter and banter continued, Jasper leaned in close. "You can't avoid this forever. And you don't have forever to find your mate. As alpha, it's your responsibility to ensure the future of the pack."

I took a swig from my beer. "Yeah. I'm aware." I didn't know why I wasted money drinking. Our metabolisms worked through the alcohol so fast, I barely felt a buzz. It couldn't come close to the rush I felt at letting my wolf out.

"You're aware mating can be fun, right? Pretty sure Nathan's well aware of—"

I punched his shoulder. "Shut the hell up." Speaking of my wolf. He growled and curled up with a huff. Letting me know he was a fan of the whole mating idea, and I was the problem here.

Jasper chuckled. "I'm just saying, you're not getting any younger, and the pack needs strong, new blood. You've got until the next Blood Moon to find your mate, or the Elders will start getting restless."

They were already restless. Keira and the rest of the peanut gallery had made their opinions on my lack of a mate clear enough. The Blood Moon, the most sacred night for our kind, was only a few months away. It was a time when the veil between worlds was at its thinnest, and the moon goddess was said to bless the unions of fated mates. If I didn't find my mate by then, the Elders would have the right to arrange a match for me, a thought that made my stomach churn.

I knew the rules, the traditions that had governed our pack for generations. An alpha without a mate was seen as weak, unable to lead and protect the pack to the fullest. And an alpha without an heir? That was unthinkable.

But I wasn't ready. The idea of being responsible for a mating bond? I was already responsible for an entire pack, and I couldn't even repair that properly. How could I take that on? A mate? Pups? No. The universe knew what it was doing. I needed to make our pack whole before I could even think about taking on something else.

As the night wore on, my packmates continued to tease and cajole me, their laughter ringing through the bar. I laughed along with them, joining in the jokes and antics, but my heart wasn't truly in it.

As the hours slipped by, one by one, my packmates began to peel off, some with their mates, others with newfound companions for the night. Eventually, I found myself alone at the bar, nursing the last of my drink.

With a heavy sigh, I settled my tab and headed out into the night. The cool, crisp air was a welcome relief from the stuffy bar.

And lucky me.

My empty apartment was waiting.

I stepped through the door and emptied my pockets on the

end table, and that's when I saw it—a message notification from Tori Campos in Chilliwack.

> Lower province pack meeting. Thursday night. Help me make some calls?

CHAPTER
THREE

EVELYN

The Amtrak train hummed beneath me as I settled into my seat, the bustling activity of Seattle's King Street Station fading behind me. I stowed my luggage overhead, but the weight on my shoulders didn't dissipate. As the train pulled out of the station, I caught a glimpse of my reflection in the window—hazel eyes shadowed with worry, auburn hair pulled back in a haphazard ponytail.

Stunning, if I did say so myself.

I slumped into my seat and stared out the window. The jagged coastline unfolded before me, the Pacific Ocean an endless expanse of gray under the overcast sky. I leaned my forehead against the cool glass, attempting to lose myself in the rhythmic clatter of the train against the tracks. It was a losing battle. My mind refused to rest.

I reached for my phone, scrolling through my recent calls

until I found the one I was looking for. *Bruce.* He'd been less than thrilled to cover my shifts for the week when I'd called in with a "family emergency." If only he knew the truth.

He hadn't put up much of a fuss, especially after I reminded him of the countless times I'd covered his ass over the summer. His penchant for late nights and pretty faces had left me picking up the slack more times than he cared to admit.

But my current predicament made Bruce's indiscretions seem trivial. I was heading back to the one place I'd sworn I'd never return—back to my pack, back to the alpha who had made my life a living hell.

Memories flickered through my mind like a twisted slideshow. Dark eyes filled with malice, claws digging into flesh, the coppery scent of blood heavy in the air. I shuddered, pushing the images away. It had been five years since I'd left Kitimat, but the scars—both physical and emotional—still stung.

I turned my attention back to my phone, desperate for a distraction. A news headline caught my eye: "Another Unexplained Disappearance in Northern BC." My breath hitched. It wasn't the first story of its kind I'd seen recently. People vanishing without a trace, search parties turning up empty-handed. The humans chalked it up to the vast wilderness, to the dangers of the untamed forest or inexperienced tourists. But I knew better.

Shifters had lived among humans for centuries, hiding in plain sight. We looked like them, talked like them, blended into their world seamlessly. But there were signs if you knew where to look. Unexplainable things that hinted at something more lurking beneath the surface. The darkness we fought on their behalf.

I scanned the article, my heart sinking with each word. A hiker gone missing near Terrace, his campsite found abandoned, his supplies untouched. It was a story I'd heard before, but not since I was a kid. A rogue shifter or something more sinister?

I set my phone aside, my mind spinning. Was this what had led to Callista's disappearance? Had she stumbled upon something she shouldn't have? Trusted the wrong person?

The train pressed on, and I closed my eyes, steeling myself for what lay ahead.

THE CHANGE in motion jolted me from a restless sleep. As the train pulled to a stop, I gathered my belongings and stepped onto the bustling street. The fresh air filled my lungs, a bittersweet reminder of the home I'd left behind. Seagulls circled overhead, their cries mingling with the chatter of tourists and locals alike.

Peak season in Vancouver. A perfect time to blend in...or get lost.

I wove through the crowd, my senses on high alert. It had been over a year since I set foot in this province, but the memories came flooding back with each step. The laughter of my packmates, the thrill of the hunt, the sense of belonging that had once filled my heart. But those days were long gone, shattered by the cruelty of an alpha who cared more for power and control than for his own people.

I made my way from Pacific Central Station to False Creek, my stomach grumbling. A small fish and chips stand caught my eye, and I joined the line of hungry patrons. As I waited, I scanned the faces around me, searching for any sign of recognition. But the people of Vancouver went about their lives, oblivious to the world that lurked just beyond their sight.

"What can I get for you?" The man behind the window looked like he'd just gotten off a rafting trip in Jasper.

"Fish and chips, please. And a Coke."

He nodded, setting to work on my order. I leaned against the counter, my gaze drifting to the harbor beyond. Boats bobbed in the water, their hulls painted in bright colors. A group of children tossed bread to the eager gulls, their laughter carrying on the breeze.

For a moment, I allowed myself to imagine a different life. One where I wasn't burdened by the guilt of leaving my pack, where I could live among the humans and pretend to be one of them. But the illusion was shattered as quickly as it had formed. I was a shifter, bound by duty and blood. There was no escaping that, no matter how far I ran or how deep I shoved my emotions.

I paid for my meal and found a bench to sit and eat. The fish was crispy, the chips hot and salty. I savored each bite, knowing it might be my last decent meal for a while. Where I was going, I wouldn't be free to saunter into the cozy pubs or stand in the open waiting for a food truck.

As I finished my lunch, I pulled out my phone and called a rideshare. It was a long drive to the Kitimat territory, and I wasn't in the mood to navigate the winding roads myself. The car arrived a few minutes later, a sleek black sedan with a friendly driver at the wheel.

"Headed north, eh?" he asked, his eyes crinkling at the corners.

"Yep." I slid into the back seat after checking the license plate. I wasn't in the mood for small talk.

He nodded, merging into traffic. As we left the bustling streets of Vancouver behind, the landscape morphed. Towering trees replaced skyscrapers, their branches reaching toward the sky. The air grew crisper, the world quieter.

"Beautiful country out here." The driver's voice broke the silence. "You're lucky if you call this place home."

I smiled wryly, my gaze fixed on the passing scenery. *Lucky.* The word made my face pinch. "It's a special place. But it's not my home." I kept my voice neutral. "The people here, they're connected to the land in a way most folks can't understand."

The driver nodded, his eyes alight with passion. "That's what I love about this part of the world. The respect for nature, the desire to protect what we have. It's not like that everywhere, you know? Some people, they just want to take and take until there's nothing left."

"You're not from BC?"

He shook his head. "Chicago."

I nodded, shifting slightly so he couldn't see my face in the rearview. His words struck a chord within me, echoing the very mission of the shifters. We were the guardians of this land, the protectors of the delicate balance between man and nature. It was a heavy burden, one I had once been proud to bear.

But that was before. Before the threats, the violence, the fear that had driven me from my home and my pack. I closed my eyes, memories flooding back unbidden.

The cruel smile of my alpha as he towered over me, his claws digging into my skin. The whispers within the pack when I dared assert that Nathan hid something dark behind his hero facade. And then, the moment I knew I had to run, had to leave everything I loved behind—

"You alright, miss?" the driver asked, his voice laced with concern. "You look a bit pale."

"I'm fine," I lied. "Just tired. Thanks."

He nodded, understanding in his eyes. "Well, you just sit back and relax. I'll get you where you need to go."

As the car wound its way deeper into the wilderness, I couldn't shake the feeling that I was heading toward something I wasn't prepared for. The shifters needed my help, that much was clear. But at what cost? And would I be strong enough to face the demons of my past in order to protect the future of my kind?

Only time would tell. For now, all I could do was watch the trees blur past the window and pray that I could find Callie before Nathan returned home.

I watched the kilometer markers whizz past until the car slowed to a stop. My brow furrowed in confusion. This wasn't the meeting point I'd agreed upon with Blake. In fact, this wasn't even Kitimat territory.

"I think there's been a mistake." I leaned forward. "This isn't where I'm supposed to be."

He inspected the app on his phone. "So sorry, but this is the address you gave me."

I groaned, realization dawning. In my haste to input the destination, I must have accidentally selected the Tim Horton's at the north end of Black Lake. Easy to do when there was one on every corner. Now, instead of being on the cusp of Kitimat land, I was still a ways out, with a long walk ahead of me.

"Any chance you can head up to Kitimat?"

He shook his head apologetically. "Sorry, I've got another ride pinging me. I'm so far out, I've got to take it, or I won't get a fare on the way back into Vancouver."

I nodded and grabbed my bag, then pushed out of the car. "My fault. Thanks for the ride."

The driver smiled, his eyes crinkling at the corners. "No worries. Have a great night."

I nodded, shouldering my bag and heading toward the Tims. If I was going to make this trek on foot, I needed caffeine.

As I reached for the door, it swung open, and I stumbled back. I looked up to find myself face-to-face with a man I hadn't seen in years. "Rowan," I breathed, recognizing him instantly despite the years that had stretched between us.

His towering frame commanded the space around him. Our eyes met, and time seemed to slow. He was older, broader, but those piercing blue eyes were unmistakable—even after all these years.

A tentative smile teased at my lips, but it faltered as his expression twisted into something unreadable. Flustered, almost angry.

"Evelyn?" His voice was brusque, the undercurrents of authority clear as crystal. Memories swirled in my head, of us as kids, scampering through the forest before the schism that tore our packs apart.

But now, his scent told me exactly who he was.

He was an alpha. His stance, the set of his jaw, the barely contained power rippling beneath his skin, all screaming his rank. And I, despite everything, still recognized the invisible threads of hierarchy that bound us.

I opened my mouth to respond, but the words died on my lips. There was something in his expression, a flicker of emotion that I couldn't quite place. *Anger? Fear? Disgust?*

Before I could contemplate it further, he pushed past me, his shoulder brushing mine as he stalked toward the parking lot. *Rude, much?*

I shook my head, trying to dispel the uneasy feeling that had settled in my gut. I didn't care what he thought of me, but he'd certainly recognized me. He and Nathan were the antithesis of bosom buddies, but I didn't need anyone spreading rumors about me showing up in town.

I stepped into the warmth of the Tim Hortons, the scent of coffee and baked goods enveloping me like a comforting hug. My thoughts clouded as I stared at the line of maple donuts.

Rowan. An alpha now. In our world, alphas were born leaders, strong and dominant, while betas and omegas fell into line behind them. But there was something else about Rowan, something that set him apart from other alphas I'd known. A darkness in his eyes, a tension in his jaw. It was as if he carried the weight of the world on his shoulders.

I shook myself mentally. I couldn't afford to get distracted by ghosts from my past. I had a job to do, and I intended to see it through.

I paid for my coffee and bagel and started my trek. It didn't take as long as I thought. The weather was good, and I kept off the main roads. As soon as I crossed over, a familiar scent hit me—the earthy, musky aroma of my pack—and I nearly dropped to my knees.

Tears stung my eyes as I pressed on to the correct coffee shop. My heart quickened as I saw them waiting for me, their faces etched with a mixture of relief and worry.

Blake stepped forward first. His muscular frame engulfed me in a hug that had no business feeling as good as it did. "Evelyn," he murmured, his voice rough with emotion. "Thank you for coming."

I pulled back, searching his green eyes. "Of course. I came as soon as I could."

Celeste, Blake's mate, was next. She cupped my face in her hands, her touch gentle and maternal. "We didn't know who else to turn to. We still don't have another tracker."

I swallowed hard, trying to ignore the lump in my throat. "Tell me everything."

We went straight to their car, away from prying eyes and ears. I sat in the back, my coffee forgotten in my hand as I focused on Blake and Celeste.

"She was acting strange before she disappeared." Blake started the car and pulled out of his parking spot, his brow furrowed. "Secretive. Distant. It wasn't like her."

Celeste nodded, her sandy hair catching the sunlight. "She'd been spending a lot of time alone in the woods. We thought maybe she'd met someone, but..."

"But what?" I prompted gently.

"She seemed scared," Blake admitted. "Like she was running from something. Or someone."

A chill ran down my spine. In our world, there were plenty of things to be scared of. Rival packs, rogue shifters, humans who would never understand our way of life.

"Did she say anything else?" I asked. "Anything that might give us a clue as to where she went?"

Celeste shook her head, her eyes shimmering with unshed tears. "Nothing. She just... vanished."

Blake pulled onto their street, and my head snapped to the end of the block. My house. *Or the house Nathan wanted to be mine.*

I kept my head down as we hurried inside, and I excused myself, straight into Callista's room. The scent of wildflowers, so uniquely hers, enveloped me as I stepped inside. Everything looked just as she would've left it—the bed neatly made, a stack of books on her nightstand, a sweater draped over the back of her chair.

But as I began to search, opening drawers and rifling through papers, a nagging sense of unease grew in the pit of my stomach. This was Callista's space, her sanctuary. It felt wrong to invade it, even if it was for her own good.

I was about to give up when a glint of metal caught my eye. Tucked in the back of her closet, half-hidden beneath a pile of clothes, was a small wooden box with a metal combination lock. My heart raced as I pulled it out, the weight of it heavy in my hands.

The lock opened easily beneath my trembling fingers. Already turned to the correct numbers, which made the whole thing seem pointless. As I lifted the lid, a gasp escaped my lips.

Inside, nestled on a bed of velvet, was a silver dagger. The blade was honed to a wicked point, the handle intricately carved with symbols I didn't recognize. It pulsed with an energy that made my wolf stir within me, hackles rising. I hadn't felt her in so long.

This wasn't just any dagger. It was a ceremonial blade, the kind used in ancient rituals and blood oaths. The kind that could kill with a single strike.

And it was the last thing I ever expected to find in Callista's possession.

CHAPTER

FOUR

Rowan

The moon hung heavy in the sky, a silent guardian as I pressed the phone to my ear. The first ring echoed like a drumbeat, quickening my pulse. I needed to catch Mara of the Riverbend Pack, and I'd already tried three numbers.

"Rowan," Mara's voice was brisk, tinged with the wariness of an alpha who had weathered many storms. "This is unexpected."

"Don't worry, I didn't want to talk to you either, Mara." I leaned against the cold railing of the balcony. That was the truth. After going into town to talk with Tori, the pack meeting should've been taking up all of my brain space.

But it wasn't. Not even close.

Why the hell was Evelyn Berry in Black Lake? I hadn't seen her since we were kids, but the two of us had history. Enough

29

that it made me sick to my stomach when I heard she was with Nathan. Sicker when I heard rumors she'd left Kitimat Pack.

Mara laughed. "Let me guess, Tori bribed you?"

"Wait, there were bribes on the table? I should've held out." Somehow I stayed present in our conversation even though my wolf was becoming unbearable. *Find her.* He was commanding me for the first time since I rose to alpha, and I didn't like it.

Mara sighed. "Let me save you the trouble. I know what this is about, and Kitimat isn't our responsibility."

"Saw that coming, but it's not me you have to answer to. I'm just the messenger this time."

"Right." Mara clicked her tongue. "I'm going to kill Tori."

"Can I watch?"

She huffed a laugh. "Tomorrow? Seriously? She couldn't even give us a day's lead time?" Before I could argue that we'd both been trying to catch her since Tuesday, she continued, "Sorry, that was in bad taste. I'm not saying I'm happy with the disappearances."

"None of us are. I understand your frustration, though."

There was a short pause. "That was surprisingly...validating of you. Did you go and mature on me, Steele?"

I laughed out loud. Mara was nearly two hundred years old. A far cry from my thirty. "I don't know whether I should be flattered or offended."

"Both. We'll be there."

As the line went dead, I set my phone on the table and pushed up from the wooden chair. I opened the fridge, the cool air spilling out to meet me as I scanned the shelves for something edible. My mind, however, was far from the task at hand. Evelyn's face kept flashing before my eyes—her fierce determination, the way she moved with purpose and grace. I grabbed a leftover steak, the scent of it filling the kitchen, but even that couldn't distract me.

My thoughts drifted back to a day long ago, back when life seemed simpler. We had been teenagers, and there was that day at the creek. I could still see the sun dappling through the trees, the water sparkling as Evelyn had laughed, splashing me playfully. She had been so full of life, her auburn hair catching the light as she teased me mercilessly about my clumsy attempts to skip stones. I could almost hear her laughter, a sound that had always made something inside me stir.

"Can't even skip a stone, eh, Steele?" she teased, her eyes twinkling with mischief.

"Hey, I'm more of a boulder kind of guy," I shot back.

I'd picked up the biggest hunk of rock I could manage and dropped it close enough that the splash drenched her from the shoulders down. She lunged at me then, and even though I was faster, I let her catch me. I let her splash me back.

I could almost feel her fingers wrapped around my forearms. The scent of her sun-kissed skin mixed with coconut sunscreen...

I blinked, realizing I was standing stock still in front of the fridge with barely enough blood above my waist to keep me upright. I cursed under my breath and adjusted myself, then walked to the air fryer like I'd just gotten off a horse.

My wolf would've been laughing had it been physically possible. I rolled my eyes and threw the steak onto the metal rack. *I don't know what you're so pleased about*, I shot back. If he wanted to mate, Evelyn was the last person we should be getting involved with.

Those moments of sneaking glances at her soaked t-shirt were long before everything had changed. Before Nathan Black had reared his ugly head. Nathan—an abusive, power-hungry alpha who had twisted our pack dynamics with his manipulative games.

My wolf growled at my train of thought. Nathan had been a nightmare. Under his so-called leadership, the pack had been torn apart. I remembered the fear in everyone's eyes, the way Nathan had ruled through intimidation and brute force. He had taken a sick pleasure in breaking those who dared oppose him, Evelyn included. She had suffered more than most, her psi abilities making her a target for Nathan's cruelty. My blood boiled just thinking about it, my wolf pacing within me, wanting to tear something—or someone—apart.

He'd come to power during the last moon of that harrowing year. Nathan had challenged my father, the former alpha of Black Lake, in a brutal fight for dominance. I had watched, helpless, as my father fell, the life draining from his eyes as Nathan claimed the title of alpha. That moment had shattered me, but it had also ignited a fire within me—a burning need to protect my pack and avenge my father.

But Nathan's hatred for me had deeper roots.

A new memory flooded my head, unbidden.

Fir branches brushing my arms. Cool summer night air. The squelch of detritus under my boots as I walked through the woods back to my house from a twilight dip in the lake.

"Stop it! They said Lana was meeting me here, please—"

A young girl's voice cut off with a yelp, and I started running.

I found Nathan pinning Court to the ground. She kicked and struggled, but he was twice her size. I didn't even think. Fury surged through me as my bones cracked and reformed, fur sprouting as I dropped to all fours, a feral growl ripping from my throat. Nathan turned, eyes widening in surprise, but it was too late. I lunged, my powerful body colliding with his and sending him sprawling to the ground, his head snapping back against a tree trunk.

Court scrambled up from the ground, screaming as she ran back in the direction of town. Nathan snarled, his own wolf fighting to the surface. He shifted as he jumped up, landing heavily on his paws, but I was already on him.

She's barely fifteen, asshole! I screamed into his head.

Nathan twisted violently. *Since when do you care who I—*

My teeth sank into his shoulder, the taste of blood spurring me on. He bucked, managing to throw me off, but I landed on my feet, ready for the next attack.

We circled each other, his amber eyes filled with hate and fury. He lunged first, aiming for my throat, but I was faster. I dodged and snapped at his hind leg, feeling the satisfying crunch of bone. He howled in pain, but the fight wasn't over.

Nathan's wolf was massive, all muscle and rage, but he was sloppy, driven by rage rather than strategy. There was plenty of that to go around.

He came at me again, and that time I let him get close. Too close. He thought he had me, jaws wide to crush my neck, but I dropped low and launched myself upward, catching him off guard. My claws raked across his belly, sending him crashing to the ground with a yelp.

I pounced, pinning him beneath me. His eyes were wild, desperate, but he couldn't shake me off. I bared my teeth, my wolf's growl a deep, rumbling threat.

Yield. Asshole, I growled.

Nathan struggled, his pride fighting against the inevitable. I pressed down harder, my claws digging into his flesh. He whimpered, the sound so pathetic, I wanted to put him out of his misery. But we were only seventeen. He'd been my best friend growing up, and then something had changed. He'd grown distant. Defiant.

I stepped back, my body still tense, ready for any trick. But Nathan remained on the ground, defeated. I shifted back to human form, standing tall over him. *Overpowering human females will never make you alpha. Get the hell out of here.*

THOSE WERE the words that echoed in my head. I thought they'd help him. Make him want to be better. Instead, they'd been the fuel for his challenge.

Nathan's reign didn't last long. His cruelty bred dissent, and it wasn't long before whispers of rebellion started circulating. Fueled by the desire to restore order and justice, I gathered my most trusted pack members. We trained in secret, planning every detail meticulously, but never had the chance to put our plan into action.

Nathan had his own secrets. In the middle of the night, he and half our pack left. Went north. In their stories, I was the dissenter. The rebel. Nathan, their savior.

The air fryer dinged, and I grabbed a plate. Had Evelyn gone willingly? Had she been his mate? My wolf's hackles rose at the thoughts, a mixture of protectiveness and something deeper stirring within me.

I slapped the meat on the plate, grabbed a fork and steak knife, and stalked back to the table. My phone stared up at me as I shoved the first bite into my mouth and chewed. I swallowed and picked it up.

Maybe there was one more phone call I needed to make.

CHAPTER
FIVE

Evelyn

Late afternoon sunlight filtered through the gauzy curtains, making the bed look like something straight out of heaven. I blinked, my heart quickening with an urgency that jolted me fully awake. I swung my legs over the edge, the floorboards cool under my bare feet. The silence of the room pressed in on me, and I flipped over my phone to check the time.

Four o'clock. *What the hell was wrong with me?* I'd wasted hours I could've been searching for more clues, and now the day was nearly over.

I wrapped my fingers around the hilt of the dagger resting on the nightstand and shivered. The metal was cold no matter how long I held it, and it felt like air from a freezer was snaking up my arm as I strode toward the door. My wolf rumbled deep within me.

She sensed it, too. Of course, she did. I stopped with my hand on the brass door knob and closed my eyes.

"Just for a minute," I whispered, then drew a deep breath and allowed my wolf to lift closer to the surface. I couldn't do this without her, but the idea of letting her loose sent ice slipping down my spine.

If humans were unpredictable and erratic after experiencing trauma, a wolf was a wildfire. I'd tried to let her out shortly after arriving in Seattle, but after she caught sight of movement and nearly killed a man out walking with his dog, I had to lock her down. She was too volatile. And I was too much of an emotional mess to take the reins.

We'd settled into homeostasis for a time, but the past six months, she hadn't been thrilled about our arrangement. I couldn't blame her, but while I felt plenty of guilt over locking her up, I couldn't risk losing control again.

That was before Callista went missing. Now we were going to have to figure out how to work together.

As my wolf ascended, I gritted my teeth at the torrent of sensation. My senses sharpened in a snap. The smells of the world became more pronounced, more nuanced. Tears stung my eyes as I tried to settle my breathing while my black-and-white world exploded into color.

"Easy," I murmured, striving for control. Embracing my full shifter abilities meant unleashing my wolf, and the thought made my knees knock. The beast within me was no longer just a part of my identity. She was a liability. A wild card I couldn't afford to play recklessly.

As she surged forward, the memory of that night flashed through my mind—a blur of fur and fangs, and Nathan's eyes, darkened with something I couldn't decipher. Betrayal or protection? The line had blurred, and my trust had shattered along with it. He had wounded us both, yet it was my wolf who bore the deeper scar, the one that festered and threatened to drive her into a frenzy.

I shook my head, trying to dislodge the image, but another took its place. *Rowan Steele.* Alpha. What? Why was she focusing on him? Sure, I'd thought about him a couple of times since seeing him yesterday and...fine, yes, he had appeared in my dreams last night, but that was normal, wasn't it? Seeing someone from my childhood after years apart was bound to mess with me. *But why was she paying attention?*

As if on cue, my wolf surged forward at the thought of him, drawn to his strength like a moth to flame. I suppressed a shudder, feeling the power of her longing.

"Stop it," I scolded, pressing my hand harder against the door. "I get that you're horny, okay? But we're here for Callista, not tail." Even as I said it, my stomach swooped. Tail did sound nice...

I groaned, forcing my eyes closed. "We can discuss that later," I hissed. Maybe I had locked down too hard, but jumping into bed with someone here was not an option. And *Rowan Steele?* Hell, no. He was an alpha, and not only outside my pack but the leader of the one pack that had ousted us. Rowan hadn't led Black Lake Pack then, but he used to be Nathan's best friend. The fact that he was their alpha now? I knew exactly how Nathan and the rest of Kitimat Pack would feel about that.

Even as that knowledge slammed into me, it hadn't kept me from noticing *all* of him in those thirty seconds. His pale blue eyes. The stubble on his chin. The energy zipping under his skin that made me wonder if he'd locked things up just as much as I had...

"Shiiiit, can you focus, please?" I gripped the door handle until my knuckles turned white, trying to think about anything other than the burning in my midsection.

Finally, I zeroed in on Callista's scent, teasing it apart from the myriad others that filled the room: the pine-scented soap she favored, the tangy residue of old tea in a cup on her nightstand, the underlying musk that was all wolf. Closing my eyes, I followed the scent trail to the window, pushing it open to let the crisp air of northern British Columbia rush in. Redwood and cedar whispered in the breeze, but underneath that, the faintest trace of Callista's passage beckoned.

I leaned out, drawing in a long, steady inhale. There it was—a thin thread of her essence, pulling me toward the dense forest surrounding the town. Her path was erratic, zigzagging through the underbrush, a sign she was either in a hurry or...

I shook my head. No time for speculation. Not when every second could mean the difference between finding her safe or not. I jumped out onto the clover and stalked forward. "She went into town." My wolf locked in, and I tracked mentally first, envisioning her potential route, noting the places where her scent spiked—by a cluster of berry bushes, across the creek where we used to play as pups, near the old logging road that humans rarely traveled.

Once I had the beginning of her trail in my mind, I slipped back inside and gathered the rest of my belongings. A sturdy jacket, some provisions, and an extra pair of socks from Callie's drawers. Essentials only. I shoved everything into a backpack and trudged into Blake's study, the cold metal of the dagger pressing against my palm. Its ornate handle glinted in the soft light filtering through the blinds, casting intricate shadows on the walls. I laid it carefully onto the mahogany desk, watching as Blake and his mate, Celeste, leaned in for a closer look.

"Ever seen anything like this?" I asked.

Blake's brows furrowed as he picked up the weapon, turning it over in his large, calloused hands. "No," he admitted, a hunter's focus narrowing his green eyes. "No markings or symbols I recognize."

Celeste, her ethereal beauty always seeming so out of place in the ruggedness of our world, shook her head, her delicate fingers tracing the air above the blade as if sensing its history. "It's not from any of our known artisans or blacksmiths. Where did you find it?"

"Under her bed."

Celeste's eyes narrowed. "This was here in the house?"

The room fell silent, each of us lost in our thoughts until Blake cleared his throat, breaking the spell the dagger seemed to cast. He placed it back on the desk with a thud. "We're heading south to the lower provincial pack meeting. You could come."

My heart skipped a beat. *Pack meeting?* I couldn't show my face in town, let alone at a meeting with every lower provincial pack. The thought of it set every nerve in my body alight with resistance. The thrumming undercurrent of my wolf's instincts warned of the inherent danger in mingling with those who could tear me apart for simply existing outside their rigid hierarchy.

"Callista might have had dealings with someone from the other packs. You wouldn't have to show your face," Blake continued, unknowingly echoing my own thoughts. "You could gather information. Watch. I could take the dagger to the elders—"

"You could take it, that's a great idea. I could stay here, and you could tell me what you find."

Blake raised an eyebrow, and he didn't have to say a word. I clenched my jaw, my heart knocking against my ribs. If there were clues out there, whispers of her fate caught in the wind, we both knew I would be the one to find them. Yet the coil of dread in my gut refused to unwind.

It was risky. The mere thought of being submerged in a sea of wolves who could recognize me tightened my chest. But Callista was out there, possibly in danger, and every instinct I possessed screamed at me to find her. To protect one of our own.

"Alright." I swallowed hard. "I'll do it."

CHAPTER
SIX

Rowan

I ended up getting four hours of sleep after making my calls and finally settling in for the night. Not the best, but not the worst either. Especially considering my wolf kept throwing images of Evelyn into my head. Was he that desperate?

Probably.

Definitely, yes.

Still, it'd been five seconds. I'd barely had time to register her face, and yet her scent was burned in my nostrils. I needed to run. I needed *him* to get his energy out so I could focus on work and the pack meeting that night.

The dawn had barely broken, but the woods of Northern BC were already alive with the muted sounds of the Black Lake Pack training. Our breath frosted in the chill air as we moved through the forest, a seamless unit of power and grace.

Keep up Rowan, Jasper's voice in my head cut through the morning stillness, a challenge wrapped in a wolfish smirk. His dark fur and muscled form, mercenary-like in its efficiency, darted between the towering redwoods with practiced ease.

I pushed harder, my muscles rejoicing in the exertion, feeling every bit the alpha I was. My wolf drove forward, thrilled to be let out to stretch his legs. Lana was to my right, her lean form a blur as she leaped over a fallen log, her tawny coat and tail streaming behind her like a battle flag.

Is that all you've got? she taunted. Lana talking shit only made me grin.

We were a small group that morning, but a force to be reckoned with. Jasper, unyielding and brutally honest. Lana, fierce and undaunted. Callum, a beta whose high energy was infectious. Liam and Mia, young wolves with eyes bright with determination, and Will, silent but unwavering. Each one a living testament to the potential of my pack.

As the sun crept higher, painting the sky with hues of gold and rose, we wound down, our run giving way to the simplicity of the day ahead. We transformed back to human forms, our laughter mingling with the rustling leaves as we each dressed and went our separate ways, ready to blend into the world of man.

I lingered for a moment longer, watching them go, pride swelling in my chest. This was more than a pack. It was a family, one I would protect with every fiber of my being. Which was why it hurt so much to know each of them still had open wounds from the split.

With a final glance at the sky, now awash with the light of day, I headed for town, toward the mechanic shop that bore my name. The rhythm of the pack's heartbeats still echoed in my ears as I swapped the wild freedom of the forest for grease-stained concrete and the scent of motor oil.

The clang of metal against metal sang out as I slid under the rusted belly of a pickup truck, the wrench in my hand my weapon of choice in this daily battle against wear and tear. "Rowan, Mrs. Henderson's here about that weird noise her Camry's been making," Jasper called out a half hour later, his voice echoing off the concrete walls of the shop.

"Got it." My mind shifted gears as smoothly as the transmissions I repaired. Sliding out from under the pickup, I wiped my hands on a rag and rose. Mrs. Henderson was a staple in Black Lake, her silver hair a badge of the years she'd spent watching over the town like one of its own guardians.

"Morning, Rowan." She greeted me with a smile that crinkled the corners of her eyes. "It's making that sound again. Sounds like a wailing banshee every time I take a turn."

I chuckled, the familiarity of our routine comforting. "Don't worry, Mrs. Henderson. We'll exorcise that banshee for you." My hands delved into the heart of her car, fingers deftly searching for the source of the problem. It was a dance I knew well, each step practiced and precise.

Even as I worked, the memory of Evelyn at the door of Tim Hortons drifted through my thoughts, unbidden but insistent. That brush of her hand had been electric, a jolt of lightning coursing through my veins, igniting something primal within me. The way her hazel eyes had locked onto mine, fierce and unyielding—it was intoxicating.

"Dammit," I muttered under my breath as I fumbled with a bolt that usually gave way easily. Since when did I let distractions cloud my focus? *Since her*, whispered a traitorous thought. My heart raced in my chest, my wolf pushing for my attention. I shook my head, trying to dispel the image of her auburn hair catching the light, the curve of her smile...

"Rowan?" Jasper's voice pulled me back to the present. "You alright?"

"Fine," I lied, not wanting to admit that I was anything but. I tightened the bolt with renewed determination, forcing myself to concentrate on the task at hand. Cars don't fix themselves, and packs don't run on daydreams.

"Looks like you had a run-in with a pretty serious pothole, Mrs. Henderson," I explained after diagnosing the issue. "Strut's busted. We'll have to replace it."

"Can you do it today?" Hope laced her words.

I didn't have time to add another car to the rotation, especially since we were trying to get out early for the meeting. "Of course," I assured her, my confidence returning as I spoke the language of solutions. "We'll take care of it."

As Mrs. Henderson left, satisfied her beloved Camry was in capable hands, I dove back into the work, hoping it would get the crazy to leave my head. I could almost hear the rumble of my wolf, restless beneath my skin, itching to break free and find her. But I pushed it down, buried it under layers of duty and resolve. If what I'd heard was true, Evelyn was a lone wolf, untethered and unpredictable. And I was the alpha of Black Lake Pack, bound by blood and honor.

The pack needed their alpha clear-headed and sharp, not lost in a haze of what-ifs and might-have-beens. There would be time to ponder the enigma that was Evelyn Berry later. For now, there were cars to fix and a pack to lead.

As the hours passed, engines roared back to life under my hands, each repair a small victory. But even as I worked, part of me remained attuned to the whisper of the forest. To the call of my wolf becoming more insistent. The yearning was a wildfire, and I was standing in the eye of the storm, trying not to get burned.

The scent of motor oil and grease was a balm to my frayed nerves as I slid under the belly of a Ford F-150 near three o'clock, wrench in hand. But even as I focused on loosening the stubborn bolts, that same undercurrent of wildness pulsed through me, a relentless whisper that beckoned me to abandon my duties and search for her—the woman with eyes like autumn leaves.

Autumn leaves? What the hell was wrong with me?

"You're a stubborn ass." Jasper's voice cut through my concentration, the clang of his tools punctuating each word. I grunted in response, not trusting my voice as my wolf rumbled within.

"Your hands are shaking. Either you tell me what's going on or I'm kicking you out of the garage." Jasper crouched, staring at me.

I tightened the bolt with more force than necessary. The metal groaned under my grip, a testament to the strength I was barely keeping in check.

"Shit bud—"

"I'm fine." My words came out sharper than I intended. "Just got a lot on my mind with the meeting tonight."

Jasper nodded, though I could tell he wasn't entirely convinced. He clapped a hand on my shoulder as I slid out and sat, a silent offer of brotherhood that steadied me for a moment before he moved back to his own work bay.

I could tell him. I knew he'd listen and probably have good advice, but the idea of admitting what was happening inside me made me want to shove a hot poker down my throat.

Evelyn Berry. A shiver ran down my spine at the thought of her with Nathan. Had she come back to be with him? Were they fated? If so, talking to her was forbidden, a line I shouldn't even contemplate crossing. Yet here I was, fighting an urge that was becoming increasingly obvious. I needed to find her. I needed to protect her. As soon as I allowed the words to run through my head, they grew until my head felt like it would burst.

Was this what it felt like? Was Evelyn's wolf calling to me? Or had I kept my wolf so bottled up that his mating desire had taken a wrong turn and latched onto the first pretty face I had a history with?

I looked over and saw Lana had arrived along with Liam, Mia, and a few other betas. I clapped my hands together. Time to get organized. "Listen up. Tonight's meeting is crucial. We'll need to be vigilant. There've been whispers of rogue shifters near the border."

"Understood, Alpha," Jasper replied with a nod, his use of my title reinforcing the weight of command resting upon my shoulders.

"Keep your senses sharp. We can't afford any surprises."

"Always," he assured me, his gaze never wavering.

"You know your assignments?"

They all nodded, and Jasper motioned for them to go out back. His voice carried over the lot as he directed Lana in the loading of supplies into the van—maps, first aid kits, and enough food to sustain our pack through a night of deliberations.

"Make sure those crates are secure," Jasper's command cut through the din, his tone inviting no argument.

"Like I'd do anything less," Lana shot back, her sarcasm a sharp contrast to the weight of the evening that lay ahead.

I listened to them snark and finished Mrs. Henderson's Camry. As I wiped down the wheel and took out the mat guards, Finn walked in, the scent of antiseptic clinging to him like a second skin. His medical bag was slung over one shoulder, the mark of his dedication to our kind.

"Got an update from Lily." Finn's voice was low but steady. "The she-wolves are comfortable, all things considered."

"Good." My mind flicked to the pregnant members of our

pack nestled in their homes, their safety paramount in these turbulent times. "Keep me posted."

"Will do," Finn assured, clapping a hand on my shoulder in silent solidarity before moving off to check our medical supplies.

Jasper and I finished up and closed shop as the sky began to bleed into dusk, painting streaks of orange and purple across the horizon. By six o'clock, there was a line of trucks and cars behind the shop.

"Let's move out." I circled my finger in the air, and Lana, Jasper, and Callum followed me toward the truck. Liam and Mia jumped in with Will.

The clearing was a thirty-minute drive, but at the last minute, I threw Jasper the keys. He held them a moment, then nodded once.

He understood.

I needed to run.

CHAPTER

SEVEN

The door of the SUV closed with a solid thud, and I sank into the plush leather seat. I'd chosen my attire meticulously for anonymity—a hooded jacket of deep forest green, loose enough to obscure my form but fitted enough to allow for quick movement. My hair was tucked away beneath a toque, and I'd popped out the lenses on a pair of Celeste's old glasses. It felt strange having anything sitting on my nose.

"Comfortable?" Blake started the engine, and the low rumble was a soothing backdrop to the thoughts ricocheting through my mind.

"Yep," I replied curtly, trying not to dwell on the tightness in my chest.

His gaze flicked to me in the rearview mirror, those green eyes assessing. "You know, you don't have to do this alone."

48

I offered him a wry smile, though it likely didn't reach my eyes. "Lone wolf habits die hard," I shifted to peer out the tinted windows. "Besides, I need to be invisible there. If anyone recognizes me, it could spook whoever we're looking for."

"Understood." He returned his attention to the road, his jaw set in a hard line.

The silence stretched between us as the miles unfurled like a dark ribbon beneath our wheels. Nathan was still up north, which meant his second would be there. I wondered if it was still Justin. Probably. Nathan didn't make friends easily and—

My phone buzzed in my pocket. I pulled it out and read the name on the screen, then sighed as I answered.

"Hey, Bruce."

"Hey, turd licker. Listen, I have a thing next week. You gonna be back by Tuesday?"

"Ooh, you've got tickets to the barn rave? Did you buy your pacifier and chaps?"

"Tuesday, Berry." He hung up, and I rolled my eyes as I dropped my phone in my lap.

"Sounds like Seattle is...fun." Blake shot me a look, and my nostrils flared.

"It was a joke."

"I thought it sounded like a blast." Celeste beamed at me over the seat.

I forced a smile, then turned my head to look out the window. Tuesday. That gave me four days. It felt like an eternity when I thought about what Callista might be enduring. A flash when I considered how little I had to go on.

"Blake," I ventured after a time, my tone even but insistent. "If things go south, if I find something... or someone finds me, promise me you'll keep your focus on the meeting. Callista is our priority." Guilt niggled at me for not worrying about the others. Beth was missing and she was younger than me, and of course I wanted to help her if I could. Merrill, too, even if he was a little odd. But it was my friend that took up most of my mental energy.

"Of course." His grip tightened on the steering wheel. "But you're not expendable, Evelyn. Don't take unnecessary risks."

A bark of laughter escaped me, mirthless and sharp. "Since when has being a shifter ever been about playing it safe?"

He grunted, conceding the point, and I swiped open my phone, scrolling through contacts labeled with mundane human names. I tapped the number for a modest hotel close enough to the meeting location but outside Black Lake territory. If I found something tonight, I didn't want to drive all the way back up to Kitimat.

"Northwoods Inn, how may I assist you?" The woman's voice was so bright, I winced.

"Room for one. Two nights."

"Your name, please?"

"Elle Bennett." I liked that name. Better than the one I gave to my landlord in Seattle. I gave the woman a credit card and thanked her just as the SUV started to slow.

I exhaled, taking in the number of vehicles parked on the overgrown path into the trees. "Seems everyone showed up."

"The last meeting that was called like this was over ten years ago." Blake parked behind a Ford truck and pressed the button to turn off the engine. "People are scared."

I nodded. Why wouldn't they be? If someone like Callie could up and disappear?

My heart thrummed a wild cadence against my ribcage, but I quelled the urge to let my wolf surge forward. Control was paramount. "I'll head into the trees. Watch from the back."

Blake nodded, taking Celeste's arm. He held out a hand. "Do you want me to take it?"

I glanced down at my bag. I knew what he meant, but for some reason, I hesitated. Finally, I unzipped the main compartment of the bag and pulled out the dagger. I could trust him. "Let me know what you find."

Voices floated through the trees as I shoved my hands in my pockets and stalked forward. I slipped through the woods unnoticed and found a place to survey the group. I allowed my wolf to rise to the surface, and this time she felt strong. Steady. The cool night air caressed my skin, as the murmurs around me swelled.

My vision sharpened, colors became more vivid, and every sound amplified. The scents around me intensified, each one distinct and layered. I took a deep breath, sorting through the myriad smells. Pine needles, damp earth, and the faint hint of smoke from an old bonfire.

I moved silently around the edge of the gathering, my footsteps light and deliberate. I instinctively knew how to blend into my surroundings and become part of the scene. Something my parents always hated.

I felt guilt niggle at me. Were they here? The idea of being so close to them and not stopping by felt like a betrayal, but they'd made it clear where they stood. They'd turned their backs on me first.

I scanned the crowd, reading body language and sensing emotions. Each heartbeat, each flicker of unease, told me a story. Then I saw him. Justin. He stood at the periphery, his posture too rigid, his jaw clenched. By the way his chest was puffed out, I had my answer about whether he'd kept his position as Nathan's second.

My instincts flared, my wolf growling softly within me. His eyes flicked to the man next to him, and I began to weave my way through the throng, my focus narrowing on the two of them. I'd only taken three steps when my wolf surged within me, a sudden, overwhelming presence that made my vision blur and my steps falter.

I grappled for control, my breath hitching as the beast within fought to break free. It was as if a storm had erupted inside me, my senses overwhelmed by the primal force of my wolf. My skin prickled, my muscles tensed, and a low growl rumbled in my throat as I grabbed onto the closest trunk.

The bark scraped my palms. *What. The. Hell?* I had never felt my wolf react so violently, so desperately. Then, as if someone had clamped their fingers under my chin and forced my head up, my eyes snapped to the front of the crowd.

And there he was.

Rowan.

Staring straight at me through the trees.

EIGHT

ROWAN

S he was here.

Evelyn Berry hid amongst the trees, her scent slicing through the pack meeting like a beacon. My wolf clawed at the surface, nearly going feral at the scent of her.

I closed my hands into fists, pacing behind Mara and Tori as they talked and clenching my jaw with such force, I thought my teeth might crack.

This was insane. I'd run twenty kilometers to tire him out, and still, this was happening? I wanted to hit something. Scream. Anything to keep from sprinting across the clearing and slamming her up against a tree and—

"Rowan?"

I turned, panting.

Tori blinked at me, her brow furrowed. "You ready to start?"

I swallowed hard, my pulse jumping in my throat. "Is everyone here?" My voice was raw, and she nodded warily. I gave my ascent, though she didn't need it. She was the regional alpha, and while I appreciated her taking each alpha's opinion into account, this was a situation where I was happy to be ignored.

Tori climbed onto a stump we'd dragged to the top of the clearing, and heads lifted all around us. The forest, cloaked in night's embrace, hushed. I spotted my wolves to my right. A respectable showing. It seemed everyone was there besides a few she-wolves and pups.

Tori lifted her voice, beginning with what we all knew. The missing wolves. The questions we all had about whether these were still rogue attacks or whether there was some other threat bubbling under the surface.

"Unity is not a request. It's a necessity," she continued, her voice echoing off the trees. Mara, her eyes like steel traps, nodded in agreement beside her. "We cannot let old feuds blind us to the danger at our doors."

A growl rumbled through the crowd as I scanned the faces of my counterparts. The Kitimat Pack huddled together, visibly apart from the rest, their expressions grim and guarded. Nathan's absence was like a gaping wound among them—he was up north with the other alphas who'd suffered losses. Briefly, compassion flickered within me, but it was swiftly drowned by a surge of bitterness.

"How can we trust the Kitimat?" someone spat from the crowd. Murmurs of agreement rustled like leaves in the wind.

"Every loss to one is a loss to all," someone shot back.

I couldn't focus on any of it. My wolf was singularly trained on her, though I still couldn't make out her form. She was in the shadows, and she was on the move.

The undercurrent of dissent still echoed around me as I

struggled to rein in my wolf, his instincts honed on Evelyn's scent. Her presence tugged at something primal within me, binding and bewildering all at once. The certainty that had always anchored me now wavered like a flame in the wind.

I didn't realize I'd started to move until Jasper's hands clamped over my shoulders. "Rowan!" Jasper hissed, slicing through the fog of my thoughts as he yanked me aside into the shadows where the moonlight barely reached. Beside him stood Will, his expression grim. They were my friends, my brothers-in-arms, yet I surged forward, crushing them both to the trunk of a redwood.

"Does this mean you owe me ten bucks?" Will grunted, struggling against my forearm pressed against his shoulder.

My eyes locked onto Jasper. "What the hell is he talking about?"

Jasper threw his head forward, striking my temple. I reeled back, dropping them. Before I could react, he grabbed my arm and threw me back into the tree I'd had him pinned against seconds before. "Breathe, Rowan. Trust me, and breathe."

Breathing was the last thing I wanted to do. I wanted to kick the shit out of him. But something in his voice made me hesitate. This was Jasper. This was my friend. *What was I doing fighting with him at the pack meeting?*

"Yep, just like that. Another one. In and out." Jasper held me tight, and I did as he said. Three breaths later, he released me. My field of vision cleared, and I saw Will standing next to us. The din in the clearing had subsided somewhat. Tori must've found some way to douse the uprising.

"Brutal, isn't it." Will ran a hand through his hair.

I frowned, still working to fill my lungs.

He shook his head. "It was exactly like that for me. You need to get a handle on it before you start a war instead of stopping one."

"What are you jabbering about?" I snapped.

Jasper chuckled. "Rowan, for being such a smart-ass, you're a little slow on the uptake with this one."

I looked between the two of them. Will looked like he'd just survived a blood trial. Jasper's smile was a little too smug.

"Fated," Will finally said. "You found your mate." He turned and pointed behind him. "I was standing there when I saw you tearing a track in the forest floor. When it looked like you were about to bury half the wolves in the clearing to get to her, I forced Jasper to step in."

The trees started to spin. *Fated?* The past twenty-four hours snapped into surprising clarity. Evelyn's scent. The way I couldn't get her out of my head. My wolf hyper-attuned to her, trying to force himself through my ribcage when I caught a hint of her presence.

"Shit." I turned and pressed my forehead against the rough bark of the tree and instantly regretted it. It was still bruised from where Jasper had knocked me.

Jasper clapped a hand on my shoulder. "Bud, I'm having a hard time understanding why you're not over the moon about this right now. Isn't this what you wan—"

"You don't get it." I spun, nearly taking his head off with my elbow. "Sorry," I muttered.

Jasper stepped back, his knees still bent into a slight crouch. *He didn't trust me.* Hell, I didn't trust me at that moment.

"What don't I get?" he asked, more politely than I deserved.

I cleared my throat. "She can't—this isn't a mating bond I can accept. It isn't something she'll accept."

"Who is it?" Will's eyes were like cereal bowls.

I debated keeping it to myself but saw no point in hiding it from them. "Evelyn Berry."

Jasper frowned. "Evelyn…"

"Kitimat. Word is she went sigma a couple of years ago."

Jasper looked up, and that's when I knew he understood. He'd heard the rumors just like I had. Nathan choosing her at the blood moon. Her showing up in town with a black eye and bloody lip, swearing it was an accident. Her disappearing and Nathan threatening everyone in his pack, trying to get a lead on where she went.

Jasper growled. "Well shit, buddy."

My thoughts exactly.

The pull toward Rowan intensified with each step I took through the trees, my heart pounding furiously against my ribcage. I tried desperately to suppress the overwhelming attraction surging through my veins, to cage the awakening wolf inside me. Memories of Nathan and his suffocating desire for me to be his mate crashed over me in terrifying waves. I had hated every second of his attempts to claim me, to force a bond I didn't want. My wolf whimpered, cowering under the onslaught of traumatic flashes.

Then that familiar scent grounded me. *Callista.* Her unique aroma hung in the air, faint but unmistakable. My senses sharpened, the world around me falling away as I focused solely on tracking the trail. I inhaled deeply, allowing my heightened olfactory abilities to guide me, narrowing the source down to...Justin.

Fear sliced through me, cold and unrelenting. The last thing I wanted was for anyone in the Kitimat Pack to know I had returned, especially someone so close to Nathan. But I couldn't ignore this lead, not when it could bring me one step closer to finding Callista. My wolf stirred, her determination rising to match my own.

Memories of his unwavering loyalty to Nathan, his cold eyes watching me, judging me, flickered through my mind. My wolf snarled, hackles rising at the thought of confronting him. But I pushed down the fear, the instinct to run and hide, and instead followed the scent, weaving through the crowd with single-minded intensity. The trees blurred around me, faces and voices fading into an indistinct hum. My wolf pressed against my skin, yearning to break free, to hunt and chase until we had our answers. I could feel her strength flowing through my limbs, sharpening my focus to a razor's edge.

I missed this. That truth washed over me just as it had back in Callista's room. The second I'd let my wolf surface, my emotions had been overwhelming.

I dodged a tree, then slid to a halt as a hand gripped my arm, spinning me around to face him.

"Evelyn, what the hell are you doing?" Blake hissed, his green eyes flashing. "Did you see that Justin's right in front of you?"

I shook off his grip, my jaw clenching. "*Her scent is on him.* I have to talk to him, Blake. I need answers."

His gaze darted between me and Justin, a war raging behind his eyes. After a moment, he nodded, his expression hardening with resolve. "Okay. I'll distract him, get him away from the others." He took a step and looked back. "I don't like this."

With a final, meaningful look, he strode toward Justin, his shoulders squared and his head held high. He clapped a hand on Justin's back, steering him away from the group with a forced laugh and a murmured comment. Blake used to be Nathan's third. I hadn't even thought to ask him if he still held that position in the pack. I assumed since he was going behind Nathan's back to call me, there wasn't any chance. Now, seeing him and Justin chum around like old friends, I wasn't so sure.

I hung back, my heart pounding as I watched them, waiting for my moment. It didn't take long. Seconds after he passed into the shadow of the trees, Justin's head snapped up, his nostrils flaring. When his gaze locked with mine, a snarl ripped from his throat, his features twisting with rage. "You," he spat, shoving Blake aside and stalking toward me. "How dare you show your face here, after everything you've done?"

My wolf surged forward, a growl building in my chest. I fought to keep her contained, to maintain control as Justin's anger washed over me. "I'm not here to cause trouble," I said, my voice low and steady. "I just want to talk about Callista."

Justin barked a harsh laugh, his eyes glinting with malice. "You have no right to speak her name, traitor. You abandoned your pack, your alpha. Nathan should have—"

A deep, menacing growl cut through the air, silencing Justin mid-sentence. Rowan stepped forward, his powerful frame vibrating with barely restrained fury. "Watch your tongue," he warned, his voice a low rumble that sent shivers down my spine. "You will show respect to every wolf at this meeting, or you'll answer to me."

Justin's eyes widened, a flicker of fear passing over his face before it was replaced by a sneer. He straightened, squaring his shoulders as he faced Rowan. "The day I answer to you, Steele, is the day I lick my own human balls. This is between me and the traitor."

Rowan stepped closer, his body coiled with tension. Heat radiated off him, the raw power that simmered just beneath the surface. My wolf whined, torn between the desire to submit and the urge to stand her ground.

"Every wolf in the southern province is under Tori's protection until we break," Rowan growled, his eyes flashing golden. "I'm Tori's enforcer tonight. If you challenge Evelyn, you challenge me."

Evelyn. The way he said my name sent chills racing over my skin.

The air crackled with tension as they stared each other down, their wolves rising to the surface, their features sharpening, their muscles rippling beneath their skin. My own wolf paced restlessly, caught between the overwhelming pull toward Rowan and the instinct to diffuse the situation.

As Justin bared his teeth, I lunged forward. "Stop! Both of you." The last thing I wanted was to draw more attention to myself.

Rowan's gaze snapped to mine, his eyes blazing with an intensity that stole my breath. For a moment, I was lost in the depths of his stare, drowning in the primal need that pulsed between us. My skin tingled, my wolf whimpering with longing. *Why the hell did I want to go to him?* I hadn't seen him in seven years, and neither of us was a silly sixteen-year-old kid anymore.

With a shuddering breath, I tore my gaze away, focusing on Justin, still seething. "We're all here because we're concerned with the missing wolves, yes?" He didn't answer, so I pressed on. "I'm a tracker. You know this. Like I said before, I'm not here to cause trouble. I'm only here to see if I can help, and then I'll crawl back under my rock." If you can't beat 'em, join 'em.

Justin's lip curled, his eyes darting between me and Rowan. "I don't owe you anything. If you want answers, you'll have to go through Nathan. Good luck with that."

As an EMT, I had been trained to assess and treat injuries, to use my knowledge of the human body to heal and save lives. But now, as I pictured Justin's smug-ass face, I found myself imagining all the ways I could make him talk, all the pressure points and nerve clusters I could exploit to extract the information we needed.

I shook my head, disgusted with myself for even considering such tactics. I wouldn't stoop to Nathan's level, wouldn't resort to violence and cruelty to get what I wanted. There had to be another way, someone else who could help us fill in the blanks.

With a final, venomous glare, Justin spun on his heel and stalked away, leaving me trembling. I closed my eyes, fighting back the tears that threatened to spill down my cheeks. I let out a shaky breath, my mind racing as I tried to piece together the fragments of information we had gathered. Justin's reaction only confirmed my suspicions—he knew something about Callista's disappearance.

"We need to talk to the Elders." My voice was steadier than I felt. Without meeting Rowan's eyes, I whirled, grabbed Blake's arm, and stalked back into the trees.

TEN

ROWAN

The woods were a blur of green and brown, but all I could see was the flash of auburn hair as Evelyn disappeared between the trees with Blake. My chest tightened, an invisible claw clenching around my heart, and pain shot through me like I'd been physically struck. It was ridiculous—I shouldn't care who she walked into the woods with or why—but I did. More than I wanted to admit.

"Rowan," Will's voice cut through the fog of my turmoil, low and cautious. Beside him, Jasper's gaze bore into me, unyielding and sharp. They saw too much, understood the chaos roiling beneath my skin. I despised that vulnerability, that lack of control over my own emotions. An alpha should be composed—impenetrable. Yet here I was, laid bare by a lone wolf.

With a snarl, I turned on my heel, stalking back toward

where Tori and Mara waited for an update. My pack waited in the clearing, and the need to assert my authority—to reestablish order—pulsed through me. Guilt gnawed at me as I realized I had missed most of the meeting. They deserved better from their alpha.

"How did it go?" I asked, my voice gruff.

Tori stepped forward, her expression neutral but her eyes filled with concern. "Most agree with the plan."

"Good." I ran a hand over my face. "That's good."

Laughter bubbled up from a small group of our she-wolves nearby, the camaraderie among them palpable even from a distance. Mara joined in, her smile genuine as she tossed a playful jab at one of our omegas.

Tori nudged my arm. "Are you still in agreement that Black Lake will join with River Bend and Chilliwack packs? We can increase patrols, especially at our borders."

"What about Kitimat?"

Tori shrugged. "I guess we'll find out when their alpha gets back. His second wouldn't commit to anything."

Not surprising. "We can cover the eastern ridge. Chilliwack can take the river pass. Rylan," I called out to our lead scout, and he was instantly at attention. "Coordinate with Mara. Ensure there's no lapse in surveillance." His affirming nod was all the assurance I needed.

I turned again to the shadowed woods, but as I took a step, Tori caught my arm. "Don't think I didn't notice you nearly ripping Justin's throat out a few moments ago."

I drew a breath, and my jaw tensed. "We were having a conversation."

"No, Rowan, we're having a conversation. You two were having a pissing match. What the hell were you thinking? The last thing we need is another wedge between Kitimat and the rest of us."

"You think that was my intent?"

She sighed. "No, but you're not exactly an open book at the moment, so what am I supposed to think?"

Her question hit like a claw swipe. Guilt and frustration knotted within me. "It's nothing," I lied, unable to meet her piercing stare.

"Nothing doesn't cause a brawl at a pack meeting," she pressed, her suspicion as palpable as the tension between us.

"Drop it, Tori," I growled, the alpha rising in warning. But she didn't back down. She never did. Her wolf peeked through, reminding me that as the regional alpha, she had seniority here, and she would use it. "Conflict is the last thing we need," I murmured. "I'm sorry."

"Better. Next time, I'd like you standing with me, not snarling at the trees."

"I wasn't—"

"Kidding, Rowan." She clapped my shoulder and leaned in. "At some point, I hope you tell me who she is."

My eyes widened, and she laughed out loud before going to rescue Mara from being swept into a game of hide and seek.

"Does everyone know?" I snapped, mostly to myself, but Will nodded next to me.

"It's pretty obvious. At least for those of us who are mated."

"Perfect." I slammed my palm against the tree, my head still throbbing slightly from earlier. The swelling was already going down thanks to our regenerative abilities. The rest of the world talked about good genetics, but we beat humans by a stretch.

The last of my pack's shadows melded with the underbrush, their forms disappearing into the night as parents wrangled their pups and returned to their vehicles. I surveyed the clearing, a lingering sense of urgency tethering me to the spot. The forest hummed with life around us, whispering secrets on the wind that rustled through the redwood leaves.

And then I saw her. Another flash against the verdant backdrop of the forest. My breath hitched, and every fiber of my being honed in on that fleeting glimpse. It was her—it had to be. The sight of her was a punch to the gut, a call to every instinct that roared within me.

"Rowan?" Tori's voice came from the edge of the forest.

"Go," I managed, tearing my gaze away from where I'd seen her. "I'll catch up."

With a last critical glance, Tori turned, melting into the night as I fought the battle raging within me. My pack needed me. But my wolf wouldn't ignore this. If Will was right, if Evelyn was my fated mate, then I had to see this through.

"Damn it," I muttered, already feeling the bonds of duty stretch taut as I prepared to follow her trail. There was no choice—not really. Not when every part of me was already straining toward the woods, toward her.

CHAPTER

ELEVEN

"Looks like some packs are actually considering the alliance," Blake murmured, his eyes scanning the residual groups that lingered in the dark. "A unified front. It's what we need."

I nodded, unable to shake off the cloak of nervousness that clung to me. The Elders of the Kitimat Pack would be no easy quarry. Skepticism ran deep in their veins, almost as deep as their loyalty. And here I was, a defector, a lone wolf about to ask them for a favor.

I drew a deep breath. I wasn't doing this for me. I was doing this for one of their own—to help their pack. The fact that I stood here filled with self-doubt made me want to punch something.

That was what Nathan had done to me. Made me doubt myself. Made me question my own version of reality. *No.* I was making my own sacrifices to be here, and they could shove their criticism where the sun didn't shine.

"Let's do this." I nodded to Blake, and he handed me the dagger. With an imperceptible nod, he beckoned me toward a secluded alcove shielded by ancient trees. "Will they all come?" I asked.

"Only a few," Blake replied, his sandy hair catching the moonlight that broke through the canopy. "The rest have gone with Justin. They trust his judgment."

That was to be expected. I didn't know if Blake had told the elders who they'd be meeting, but I doubted he'd given them the whole truth. The way Justin had reacted earlier...I shivered. Nathan would be returning soon, and I needed to be far from Kitimat when he arrived.

A few moments later, the Elders emerged from the shadows like specters of a bygone era, their figures imposing even under the heavy cloak of night. Elder Marlowe led the procession, his silver hair cascading over broad shoulders. He carried with him an air of command that often made wolves twice his junior cower. His piercing gaze settled on me, and I could feel the weight of his scrutiny.

"The prodigal. Returned." His voice was gravelly, carrying the resonance of a growl even in human form.

"Does our alpha know of this?" chirped Elder Tara, her frame lithe and movements spry as she rounded Marlowe like a cunning fox. Her eyes twinkled with mischief, though her tone held an edge sharp enough to cut through bone.

"I'm not interested in betrayal," retorted Elder Cormac, his burly figure moving forward with a lumbering grace. The lines on his face deepened as he frowned.

"Enough," snapped Elder Keira, meeting my eyes.

She'd seen me once. In the grocery store. I'd gone out to buy apples, and Nathan didn't like returning from work to find the house empty. I'd thought I left enough time, but there was only one checker open. I was a nervous wreck, sweating through my shirt, when I started out to the parking lot. That's when I saw Keira. Next to Nathan's truck.

Keira gave me a slight nod. "Tell me why you're here, child." With one piercing look, it was as if she saw beneath my surface. She knew. They may not approve of the choices I made, but she at least understood why I'd made them.

"I'm here for Callista. For the Ash family. I know Kitimat doesn't have a tracker." *I still love my pack.* I couldn't quite say those words out loud, but I felt them. It was true. I missed this place. I missed my family and friends. But no amount of community was worth bondage.

"I found this." I drew the dagger from my coat, the blade catching the scarce light and throwing it into the Elders' faces. Their expressions shifted from skepticism to solemnity in a matter of seconds.

Cormac stepped closer, his large hand hovering over the weapon but not touching it. "Where did you find this?" he asked, his voice losing its earlier bite.

"I believe Callista had it," I replied.

The elders exchanged looks.

"Never straightforward, are you, Evelyn?" Marlowe's lips twisted into something between a smirk and a sneer. His eyes, though, remained locked on the dagger.

"Only when it serves my purpose," I shot back, feeling that familiar tickle of defiance. I was a grown-ass woman with a strong wolf. I wasn't going to allow them to treat me like a petulant child.

"Marlowe, hold your tongue," Tara chided softly, her silver hair shimmering even in the dim light. Her eyes narrowed slightly as she turned to me. "These markings," she murmured, gesturing at the intricate etchings on the blade. "They speak of old magic, of a time when the veil between worlds was thinner."

"Indeed," Cormac rumbled, his deep voice carrying an undercurrent of concern. His fingers brushed over the symbols, careful not to make contact with the steel. "I've seen similar craftwork once before—"

"Enough," Lysander interrupted, his green eyes flashing with urgency. The others fell silent, turning to him.

I waited impatiently. This was always how it was with the elders. They wanted to help the pack, but they wouldn't give up their secrets.

"This magic has made its way to Kitimat," I said. "There's no benefit to hiding what you know. Callista is out there, along with the other wolves that have disappeared. I need to find her."

Lysander pursed his lips. "We don't have the answers you seek. But if you take this to Lyra—"

Tara hissed a breath. "Wolves do not collude with witches."

"Who's Lyra?" My heart began to speed.

"Lyra Moonshadow," Keira began, holding up a hand when Tara tried again to cut in. "A witch of formidable power who fled to the northern reaches long ago. She sought solitude after a great tragedy befell her."

"Tragedy?" I pressed, sensing there was more they were hesitant to reveal.

"Her mate," Lysander said simply, and the finality in his tone told me all I needed to know about the depth of Lyra's loss. "Cursed and taken from this world. She's been alone ever since, meddling in human affairs. Her loyalty to none but herself."

"Meddling how?" I could feel my curiosity morphing into

resolve. If this witch knew anything about the dagger, I needed to find her.

"She follows *whims*," Tara said, as if it were a curse word.

"Her magic is not bound only to nature itself," Cormac said. "But if she was involved in creating this..." He shook his head. "I don't know what would compel her to do such a thing."

"Has anyone in Kitimat met her recently?" Blake asked, and I knew what he was thinking. Why would Callie have this? Callie was curious, but even I didn't believe she would have gone on a jaunt through the woods to meet a witch.

"Be careful." Marlowe said gruffly, his gaze finally leaving the dagger to meet mine. "Kitimat does not bend easily, even to the likes of witches."

It was the closest anyone had come to pretending I was still a member of the pack. My eyes stung at the corners just as a stone settled in the pit of my stomach. I didn't know what I'd been expecting, but it definitely wasn't witchcraft.

"Are you okay?" Blake asked, his voice low as we slipped away from the clearing. The moon cast dappled shadows across his concerned face.

"Fine," I lied, my voice steady despite the turmoil churning inside me.

"Everything went well?" Celeste asked as we approached the truck.

"Define 'well'," I quipped, forcing a smile that didn't reach my eyes. "We have a lead."

"Hey, that's a start." Celeste looked so hopeful, I swallowed the next words that wanted to come out of my mouth.

We took our seats, and the truck's tires crunched over the gravel as we pulled away from the wooded enclave. Blake drove in silence, his jaw set in a line that told me he too was processing the night's revelations. My fingers drummed on the windowpane, cooling against the glass.

I watched the trees blur past, their shadows melding with the night, an obsidian tapestry pierced only by the occasional glint of moonlight. The forest of northern British Columbia had always been my haven, and yet tonight, it felt like a stranger.

"Drop you at the hotel?" Blake asked, glancing at me briefly before his eyes returned to the winding road.

"Please." I nodded. I hoped they weren't offended that I wasn't staying with them for more than a night. Blake was probably relieved after what happened in the clearing. Now if Justin stopped by, Blake wouldn't have to explain why I was sitting in the living room.

Lights began to wink through the trees around us as we passed over Black Lake territory. We pulled into the hotel's parking lot, a nondescript two-story building with a fresh coat of paint.

"Thanks for the ride." I reached for the door handle.

"Of course. Call if you need anything," Blake replied, but I was already stepping out into the crisp night air. I gave a small wave and slung my backpack over my shoulder, the dagger tucked safely inside.

The hotel's lobby was empty, save for the night clerk who barely glanced up from her book as I checked in. Her disinterest was oddly comforting. I took the keycard and made my way to door 217.

Inside, the room was just as unremarkable as the rest of the building—beige walls, a bed with a quilted comforter, and a solitary painting of a lake at sunset. But it was the silence that eased my anxiety.

I shed my jacket and boots, and moved almost mechanically, washing my face and brushing through my hair. It was then that Rowan pushed his way back into my thoughts. Why had he jumped into my conversation with Justin? Did he think I couldn't handle myself?

The way he looked at me...

My blood heated just thinking about it. He was alpha of Black Lake. I had so many questions for him. Nathan had told me plenty about who Rowan was, but there wasn't much that came out of his mouth I believed anymore.

I'd spent months in Seattle trying to untangle the lies from truth. I still didn't understand why Nathan had challenged our alpha. I didn't understand why my parents chose to side with him instead of staying with Black Lake. They hadn't been willing to answer my questions then, and I doubted they'd open up now. Especially since I may as well have been a stranger to them.

I pulled back the covers and was about to slip into bed when a deafening knock shattered the fragile silence of my hotel room, jerking me out of my thoughts. My pulse spiked, the instinctual side of me rising to the fore as I sprang from the bed, every muscle tensed for action.

"Who is it?" I called, wary. But there was no response— only another urgent pounding that seemed to echo the racing of my heart.

I approached the door slowly, the grain of the cheap carpet rough against my bare feet. The hotel had felt like a safe haven moments before. Now, the four walls felt restrictive, the shadows lurking in corners suddenly too dark, too deep.

Gripping the handle with one hand, I had no choice but to reach for my wolf, letting her senses enhance my own. After what happened in the trees earlier, the idea of relying on her sent my heart into palpitations. Would she run? Fight? Try to hump something?

I closed my eyes and took my chances.

The scent under the door nearly knocked me off my feet. "Evelyn, it's me. Rowan. Can you open the door, please?"

CHAPTER

TWELVE

Rowan

After two knocks, I didn't think she was going to open the door. *Break it down.* My wolf didn't normally form words, and the impact of those nearly knocked me off my feet.

Holy shit. Keep it together. If I didn't keep him under control, we were going to end up in an overnight jail cell.

I raised my knuckles to the wood one last time, but the door creaked open. My gaze latched onto the sliver of her I could make out, framed by the doorway. Her hazel eyes were wide with what I hoped was surprise and not anger.

My wolf prowled just beneath the surface, the sight of her stirring a wildness within me that strained against the leash of control. Every muscle in my body tensed as I fought to keep the beast at bay.

And then her scent hit me. A unique mix of sweet and salty

75

that reminded me of beach trails and heather. It ignited an instinctual need that was nearly impossible to suppress. I wanted to force the door open. To press my body against hers. To ease back her head and taste her neck.

The wolf inside me wanted to claim, but I drew on every shred of self-control and stood rooted to the spot, the cool night air doing little to quell the heat that coursed through my veins. My wolf was so alive that every sound was amplified— the distant hoot of an owl, the rustle of a receipt blowing through the parking lot, the soft inhale of Evelyn's breath as she studied me.

"What are you doing here?" she finally asked, her voice a knife-edge balancing caution and curiosity. *Was she afraid of me?* That possibility gave me pause. Had I done anything that would make her think I was a threat?

No, but I didn't have to. Of course she was afraid. I was the alpha of Black Lake. What reason could I give her for standing on her doorstep besides the truth?

"I wanted to make sure you were okay." It was a piece of the truth. One I hoped wouldn't send her slamming the door in my face.

"I'm fine."

"I can't tell if that's true."

"It is."

"Well, I can't see much through this gap—"

Evelyn swung the door open, giving me a less-than-amused expression. "Satisfied? I'm all in one piece."

She was wearing boy shorts and a long-sleeved cotton shirt that draped over her hips. Satisfied didn't begin to cover it. "Can I come in?"

"Hell, no."

Fair enough. I nodded, then leaned against the door so she didn't have to hold it open. "Do you want me to beg?"

"Do alpha's do that these days? So progressive of you."

I smirked. "Not usually. But I do make exceptions."

The skin along her collarbone turned pink, and my wolf rumbled in my chest. Yeah. We both liked that a hell of a lot.

Evelyn let go of the door and took a step back. "You shouldn't be here."

"I don't see a problem with it."

Evelyn shot me a look. "You're outside of Black Lake territory."

"These are neutral lands."

"I'm not neutral, Rowan, and you know it. I'm Kitimat territory."

"I heard you didn't belong to anyone these days."

She drew an exasperated breath and crossed her arms in front of her. Somehow she looked even hotter when she was pissed. It made me want to say something else asinine just to see how much I could get her cheeks to flush.

"That's it, then? You've heard the gossip, and you're curious?"

"I've been curious about you for a long time."

She huffed a laugh. "Bull shit. I lived twenty minutes up the road for two years, and you never came to my doorstep."

This was quickly veering off the tracks, but what had I expected? To show up here and have her throw her panties at me? Yeah. Kind of. I was an alpha. I wasn't used to wolves shutting me down. "You know I couldn't—"

"You can't be at my door *now!* What's the difference?"

My wolf pressed so close to the surface, I wondered if she could see my eyes glowing. Evelyn's breathing quickened. She put out a hand and steadied herself against the wall. My eyes narrowed. I could sense her wolf there, but something was holding her back. My wolf whined, begging for a better glimpse.

"I think you know what the difference is." It was a risk, but Evelyn wasn't giving me anything to work with. If my wolf was acting like a bat out of hell, she had to be feeling something from hers. I hoped.

When I was a pup, I thought mating bonds snapped into place and you had no choice whether you complied. Now I wasn't so naive. The mating bond was an invitation from the universe—one she didn't have to take. I had to prove myself, and I only had a week, sometimes less, to do it. After that, the pull she felt toward me would lessen.

For me? It would never stop. This was my one and only.

Evelyn didn't step aside to let me in, but she didn't tell me to leave, either. That was something. "Can we talk?" My question hung between us, an offering and a plea. I watched as the wildness in her own gaze—a reflection of her inner wolf— flickered with indecision.

"I'm here for four days, Rowan. Then I'm going back to Seattle. I'm only here to help my friend."

My wolf growled, and I lowered my eyes so she wouldn't catch the anger that flashed there. I mentally stroked a hand down his smoky back. *Be patient.*

I wouldn't admit it to Evelyn, but she was right about one thing. I had heard the gossip about her and Kitimat's alpha. I *was* curious. But I didn't need her to spell it out for me. If Nathan had treated her the way everyone thought he had, it made perfect sense that she wouldn't trust me, regardless of our history.

I cleared my throat. "Right. That's what I wanted to talk about. After what you said to Justin—"

"This isn't any of your business." Evelyn put a hand back on the door, moving to push me out. That made my hackles rise.

"It's all of my business. My pack is making sacrifices to

help Kitimat and the other northern packs that are missing wolves. Not that you would know, but we're a small pack as—"

"Not that I would know?" Her grip tightened on the door, her eyes flashing.

My nostrils flared. "That wasn't a judgment. Just a fact."

Evelyn leaned closer, and her scent made me heady. "You're blocking my door, and I'd like to get some sleep. Not a judgment. Just a fact."

"Do you think you can make me move?" As soon as I said it, I regretted it. Walls slammed down behind her eyes, and her expression hardened. "I'm sorry. It was a joke. I'll leave."

She paused, and the haunted look in her eyes nearly brought me to my knees. I wanted to tell her I wasn't him, that I would never be him. I wanted to sprint away from her door and never stop running until I found Nathan Black and tore his head from his shoulders. Instead, I said, "If you want me to."

My wolf stood at attention, so focused I didn't think a scrap of fresh deer meat could tear his eyes from her.

Evelyn turned her back, and my stomach sank like the boulders I used to toss in the river. She was rejecting us. *She was rejecting me.* The pain of that realization tore at my insides as I pushed off the door, ready to take my walk of shame to the parking lot and let it close behind me.

"I found this." Evelyn's voice was soft.

I looked up, not trusting myself to speak. She held something in her hands. Something sharp. She walked slowly back toward me and held it out. I took it from her and began inspecting it, still trying to clear the hunk of granite sitting on my chest.

I tried to focus on the intricate carvings in the dagger's handle, but my vision blurred. *She wasn't saying no.* Not yet, at least. Had she understood what I was trying to say? Did she know that we were fated? If she did, she obviously wasn't impressed.

"You think this has to do with the disappearances?" I asked.

She nodded, still not meeting my eyes. "Blake and I talked with the elders. They said a witch in the woods might have more answers."

So that's what she was doing in the trees. "Lyra."

"You know her?"

"Of her."

Evelyn's brows knit together, a testament to the wariness that clung to her like armor. She'd been alone for far too long, trusting no one, relying solely on her own strength. But the path ahead was fraught with peril, and if there was one thing my position as alpha had taught me, it was that even the strongest among us needed an ally.

"I have a truck."

She finally looked up. "Congratulations."

"It's excellent on mountain roads."

She laughed and tried to shove her hands in her pockets, but she didn't have any, so instead, she took the dagger back. "I'll be fine."

It was adorable to see her discombobulated. Almost as good as when she was angry. "Doesn't Blake have a Ford? That won't cut it. You need the reliability of a Dodge—"

Evelyn put a hand on my arm and shoved just like she did when we were kids, but this time, energy shot through me like lightning. She gasped and pulled back, pretending she'd meant to tuck her hair behind her ear.

But I saw the shock in her eyes. She felt it, too. That meant there was hope. "I can get a map. One of our elders has been there." It wasn't a lie. Elder Smythe had told the whole pack about her visit with the witch. I just wasn't sure if she'd been telling the truth. "I'll get directions and provide security. I don't know if you were planning to do this alone, but meeting a witch isn't exactly a party."

Evelyn folded her arms, an eyebrow arching as if to challenge the intensity of my gaze. "Last time I checked, invitations were required for parties."

"Consider yourself cordially invited then." I grinned, and that's when I knew I had her.

Her lips twitched, betraying her amusement. "Who says I need a big, bad alpha to protect me?"

"Big and bad, eh?" I leaned closer, lowering my voice. "You haven't seen anything yet."

A spark flickered in her eyes, a silent acknowledgment of the heat that crackled between us, wild and untamed. If she was feeling the pull I was, I have no idea how she stood firm. *Maybe she wasn't feeling it.*

"Goodnight, Rowan." Her hand slipped on the door.

"Goodnight, Evs."

Her face went slack, and my wolf howled. Until that moment, I hadn't remembered I used to call her that. I turned and strode back to the stairs at the end of the walkway, forcing myself not to look back and see if she was watching.

Somewhere between losing my shit in the clearing and her door, I'd made a decision. Kitimat and Nathan Black be damned.

Evelyn Berry was mine.

I was meeting with a witch today. I repeated that sentence in my head, and it never sounded less ridiculous. If I, a supernatural creature, couldn't wrap my head around there being a witch that lived in the woods, then who could?

My wolf pawed at my consciousness, flashing yet another image of Rowan standing in the door of my hotel room. I groaned and took a cup from the TV stand into the bathroom for a drink of water. Rowan had played on repeat in my head all night long.

I think you know why it's different.

Based on the way my wolf was acting any time he was around, I had a pretty good idea of what he was alluding to. But what kind of cruel joke was this? Rowan was the worst person I could be fated to. Okay, maybe worst was the wrong word. Most complicated? Most dangerous?

Exhibit A, he was an alpha. He was powerful and wasn't used to hearing no for an answer. He had a responsibility to his pack, and there was no way he'd ever be leaving Black Lake, which led to Exhibit B. Black Lake was barely twenty kilometers from the heart of Kitimat territory. Nathan was the alpha there, and he thought he had a claim on me, though I had plenty of four letter words at the ready for the day he tried to enforce that.

I wanted to believe Nathan had forgotten about me, that he'd moved on to some other unsuspecting she-wolf flattered by his love bombing. But I knew that wasn't true. It would never be true.

That was due to Exhibit C. Nathan hated Rowan Steele. It had been five years since our packs split, and before I left, he was still explosive when anyone mentioned Rowan or Black Lake. It wasn't hard to understand why.

Rowan was a friend to me and Nathan, and he'd only taken over after Nathan challenged his father and left. Nathan didn't see it that way. The fact that Rowan didn't follow him to Kitimat was all the evidence he needed.

On top of that, I *chose* to leave Nathan. After he'd made it clear to the entire pack that I was his. Nathan wouldn't forget that, and he certainly wouldn't forgive. If he found out I was here? With Rowan?

I shuddered at the thought and reached for my toothbrush. *But I was here with Rowan, wasn't I?* He'd been at my hotel room last night.

Had I given him permission to come with me today?

Not exactly. But not...*not* exactly.

Still. When he was around, my wolf seemed to be more steady. I was beginning to trust that she wasn't going to rip someone's head off unexpectedly.

What did that mean? Wasn't it a thing that when you got

out of one terrible relationship you were extremely likely to jump into another? Was wolf psychology the same as humans?

I paused by the door, taking a deep breath. The thought of relying on another alpha knotted my stomach. Sure, Rowan was funny. Nice. Adorable, even. But power transformed alphas, twisted them into beings who saw loyalty as a resource to exploit. I would not fall under the sway of any wolf's command again, especially an alpha.

All of it was impossible. Yet rehearsing that in my head did nothing to settle my wolf. That was a problem. I needed her for tracking, and then I needed her to take a backseat. The more I was around Rowan, the less she seemed willing to fade away like she had in Seattle.

With one last glance at the room that had been my refuge, I pushed the door open and stepped outside. The cool morning air kissed my cheeks, but my tranquility shattered when something smacked into my shins, sending me backward into the door.

I cursed, my hand instinctively reaching for the knife strapped to my hip before recognition hit. "Rowan?"

Rowan Steele unfolded himself from where he lay sprawled at my feet, startling me into a defensive stance.

"What the hell are you doing?" I hissed.

Rowan straightened up, towering over me with those piercing blue eyes and dark hair disheveled like he'd been... well, like he'd been sleeping against my door. His grin was sheepish. "Hey. I got here early. Didn't want to make you late."

"How early?" I scoffed, eyeing the leaves clinging to the same clothes he'd been wearing the night before.

"Early." He brushed off his jacket.

I pursed my lips. "Were you sleeping here outside my door?"

Rowan yawned and covered his mouth. "I may have nodded off."

I shook my head and started toward the stairs. "Unbelievable."

"You're mad?" Rowan's steps were heavy behind me.

"Annoyed would be the better term." The soles of my boots reverberated on the metal steps as I descended to the parking lot.

"Justin looked like someone pissed in his pop last night. I was worried he might do something."

I spun as I reached the pavement and had to look straight up since Rowan was still two steps up on the staircase. "Blake was the only person who knew where I was staying, and he wouldn't tell Justin."

Rowan raised an eyebrow and glanced back up toward my door. I swallowed hard. "Okay, fine, yes. Justin could've followed us here, but he didn't."

"But he could've."

I let out an exasperated breath. "Don't you have a pack to take care of?"

The rumble of an engine sliced through the morning stillness, and I turned just as Blake rolled up in his battered old truck, kicking up a cloud of gravel and dust. Rowan dropped to the ground next to me, his shoulders tense.

"Why is Blake here?" Rowan's voice was gruff.

"It's his sister who's missing. Didn't we talk about taking his truck last night?"

Rowan shot me a look, his eyes dark. I stifled a grin.

Blake cut the engine and stepped out, his muscular build momentarily outlined against the glare of the early sun. He frowned as he caught sight of Rowan standing next to me. "Did he—?" Blake looked between the two of us. "Evelyn, did you—?"

"Good morning, Blake." I stomped toward the truck and hopped into the backseat. "You two can discuss what I did or didn't do on the drive. Sound good?" I slammed the door closed.

Blake stared at Rowan a moment longer, then retreated to the driver's seat. Rowan got into the passenger seat a moment later, his frame filling his side of the cab.

"I can't have him in here, you know that." Blake's voice was low.

"He has our directions, Blake. And he's just as concerned about these disappearances as we are," I countered. Blake had been at the meeting just as I had. He'd heard how the packs wanted to band together.

Blake's jaw tensed, and Rowan put an arm up on the back of the seat. "I can wipe down the truck for you after we get back. So nobody smells me on your leather."

I held my breath. It was harder to keep my wolf from reacting to his scent when we were in such close quarters. She whined, and Rowan turned his head to look at me. *He couldn't hear her, could he?* We weren't pack mates, but truth be told, I knew nothing about mating bonds. Not that I'd accepted one, and not that I *would* accept it, but what if there was something I didn't understand?

"Which direction?" Blake started the engine.

"East." Rowan snapped, his gaze still fixed on Blake as if daring him to say more.

This was going to be a long drive.

THE DENSE CANOPY of the northern forest blurred past us as Blake's truck jostled along the rugged trail.

"Your family had a chance to make things right," Blake

grumbled from the driver's seat, his eyes flicking to Rowan. "Nathan challenged fair and square, but your lot just couldn't let go."

They'd been sending subtle jabs since we left the highway, and now they weren't mincing words. The conflict made my wolf lie down with her head on her paws, but I couldn't bring myself to stop them. These were questions I had, too. Better Blake bring it up than me.

Rowan gave a sardonic laugh. "Is that the story he tells? At least he's consistent."

"What is that supposed to mean?"

Rowan's jaw tensed. "It means he's always going to spin things to his benefit. What I can't understand is why you'd believe it."

"I'm living in the aftermath, Steele. You pushed us out."

"False." That word felt like a prelude to a storm. "We recognized Nathan as alpha, but he'd burned too many bridges. When he realized he wasn't going to be able to keep control, he poisoned anyone he could and left. *I'm* living in the aftermath."

"You think I'm an idiot? Just followed him blindly?"

"No, I think he's damn good at making people see what he wants them to see."

That hit too close to home. I leaned forward from the backseat. "You know, if you two keep this up, I'll have to sit between you."

Rowan's blue eyes met mine, and I felt it—the pull of his wolf to mine, an invisible thread tugging at my senses, stirring something deep within me. "There's room." He patted the seat next to him.

"Shut the hell up. Are you shitting me?" Blake pulled over to the side of the road, and even though I was buckled, I slammed forward but didn't hit the seat.

Rowan was halfway over his headrest, bracing my shoulder

with one arm and cupping my face with the other. "Ash, I'm going to—"

"She's your *mate?*"

"No!" I yelled at the same time Rowan growled, "Yes." I slapped his hands off me and pressed myself against the seat. His hands left streaks of heat across my skin.

Blake turned to look at me. "This can't happen."

"Don't you think I know that?" I struggled to catch my breath.

"If Nathan finds out—"

"If Nathan finds out, he can deal with me." Rowan's eyes were so bright, they shone. His wolf pressed forward, his power radiating through me, and that's when my hands started to shake.

No. I started to hyperventilate. "Shit," I hissed, scrambling for the red button to release my buckle. "Shit, shit—"

"Evs—"

"Do *not* call me that!" I shoved the door open and dropped to the ground just as my wolf burst forward, and I shifted for the first time in two years.

On the side of the highway.

At 9 am on a Friday.

CHAPTER

FOURTEEN

I chased after Evelyn through the dense forest. Her wolf was a blur of speed and panic, her scent a wild mix of fear and desperation, and my wolf surged with the need to protect her.

We came on too strong, bud, I chastised. As usual, my wolf didn't understand the definition of the word 'chill.' I loved him for that. But when he got his mind set on something, keeping him from it was like trying to drag a Great Dane by a length of twine.

I threw my consciousness toward the blur of roan fur flashing through the trees ahead of me. *Evelyn, stop.*

She stuttered a step, and I silently celebrated. We could talk to her. I'd never spoken with someone outside of my pack in wolf form, but somehow, I knew it would work. I could sense her wolf almost as acutely as I could sense my own. It was disorienting, and yet it filled me with such intense emotion, I thought I'd split at the seams.

Evelyn, please, I tried again, and that time I caught a response.

I can't do this. I need to find Callista. Her voice was fragmented. Chaotic. It reminded me of the first time our adolescents joined us on runs. I pushed harder, my paws digging into the earth as I closed the distance between us.

She was fast, but I knew these woods like the back of my hand. I could sense her inner turmoil, the raw pain and fear that drove her forward. Then color flashed in my mind, and I nearly sideswiped a Lodgepole Pine.

What the hell was that? Another image, this time with a face I recognized. Nathan Black, his eyes dark, stalking toward us.

These were memories. Her memories. Through whatever bond we'd begun to form, I could feel them pressing in on her, the horrific images she was trying so hard to outrun. Her wolf's stride faltered, and I took the chance to close in further, only to have to change course as another wolf appeared at my flank.

Blake. I'd never seen his form before, but by the worry in his eyes and the fact that we were both running the same direction, I had no doubt it was him.

Evelyn slowed. Something was passing between the two of them, and my wolf growled at the realization that Blake had been able to get through to her when we hadn't.

They were old friends. Pack mates. Even if Evelyn was convinced she'd left our world behind, her wolf was proving she wasn't satisfied to stay hidden forever.

Evelyn finally stopped at the creek ahead of us, panting hard. Blake and I stopped next to her. I wanted to shift back so I could hear what they were talking about, but none of us had any clothes. I doubted standing naked in front of each other was going to make this situation any better, though we were going to have to deal with that inconvenience sooner or later. I had extra clothes in my truck, but since she'd insisted on taking Blake's tin can, that wasn't going to help anything.

I'm sorry, I sent to her. *For whatever I said or did.*

Her head turned toward me, but she didn't speak. When she turned back to Blake, I pawed at the ground.

Evelyn's wolf was trembling, her eyes wide with fear and panic. She focused on Blake and whined softly, her body tense and ready to bolt at any moment. It tore me up inside seeing her like this, but I realized at that moment I didn't know everything I thought I did. She wasn't the same wolf I'd known back when we were kids.

You didn't do anything. Her voice finally sounded in my head, and my shoulders relaxed. *I came back to help my friend. This is too much.*

Blake moved closer to her, and my wolf understood before I did. He let out a low growl as I was catching up. This was too much. I was too much. She'd come back as a tracker, and here I was telling her we were fated. Even if she felt it like I did, she'd made it clear that she wasn't planning on coming back to her pack—to any pack.

But even as her words echoed in my head, her wolf took a step toward me. I raised my head, and she immediately yielded, lowering her eyes to the ground.

Why was her wolf acting as if I was challenging her? Why was Evelyn acting as if I was a threat?

The images I'd seen earlier clicked into place.

Because her old alpha was a threat.

Her wolf sensed both my alpha energy and the beginnings of our mating bond. One she wanted. The other she did not.

But I couldn't help that I was an alpha. I couldn't help the instinct to be by her side or to protect her at all costs. But what if that was exactly why she couldn't accept this? Couldn't accept me?

Without thinking, I flopped onto the ground, exposing my belly in a show of complete submission. Her wolf's head shot up. Her eyes widened, intensely focused on my soft underbelly.

It felt like torture lying exposed like this, but I needed her wolf to understand. Yes, I was strong. Yes, I was an alpha. But I was not there to force her paw. I would not ask for trust I wasn't willing to give, and I would never—

Blake says that's embarrassing. Evelyn's wolf took a step toward me.

I kept my eyes fixed on her. *Tell Blake he wouldn't know alpha energy if it punched him in the face.*

Her eyes narrowed as her wolf did the closest thing she could to a smile. Blake stalked forward, but Evelyn nudged him with her nose.

We should go to the truck, she said.

I rolled over and stood, dwarfing both of them as I rose to my full height. Even though I wanted to lead, I let Evelyn go first. The scent of her nearly sent my wolf into a frenzy. Thankfully, neither she nor Blake looked back to see me staring at her backside.

Evelyn stopped at the edge of the trees and turned her head to Blake. I didn't have to hear their conversation to understand. We needed to shift back to our human forms, but that meant—

Blake was suddenly standing there next to Evelyn. Butt naked. I let out an amused bark, and Blake flipped me the bird without looking back.

Tell Blake 'nice ass,' I sent to Evelyn. She rolled her eyes as I sauntered up next to her and settled onto my haunches.

You can tell him yourself after he sees yours.

A part of me wanted to shift right there. Walk down the hill in front of her and let her ogle the goods, but by the way she was sending sidelong glances, I knew she already was. My wolf was impressive. All alphas were, but I'd always loved the streaks of grey that ran over my shoulders.

Blake trudged back toward us with sweatpants and a t-shirt on. He tossed up two more sets for us, then pointed at me accusingly. "Turn around, Steele. If I catch you looking, I'll run my truck into your pasty thighs."

My thighs aren't pasty, I said.

Evelyn huffed, then turned her back. I did the same, acutely aware of the shuffling sounds behind me as I shifted and dressed. My senses were still heightened from my wolf, and I could hear every inhale, every catch of her breath as she pulled on her shirt and pants.

Sweatpants were not ideal for hiding what her proximity did to me.

Blake's eyes narrowed as I casually clasped my hands in front of my crotch and walked back to the truck. "Pants are a little short." I couldn't help rubbing in the fact that I was bigger than him.

"Asshole," Blake muttered as he rounded the hood.

When the truck finally rolled to a stop at our destination, I was the first to step out.

"A mushroom farm? Really?" Evelyn dropped to the ground next to me, her boots sinking into the mossy earth. She was wearing Blake's clothes, and everything was oversized. It was adorable to see her rolled-up sleeves and pant legs, though by the way she kept fiddling with her shirt, I doubted it felt comfortable.

"Were you expecting some mystical dwelling, maybe a

woman living in the hollow of a tree?" I asked. Evelyn barely flicked a glance my way, but her cheeks stained, and the hairs on her arm prickled.

She wanted me. The problem was, her head was telling a different story. But heads were always easier to change than hearts.

"Disappointed?" Blake asked.

"Confused." Evelyn chewed her lower lip. "She's a witch, and she…just runs a business out here?"

"Everyone has to make a living." I started toward the small building. "It's not like we live in a fairytale."

"You're here, so definitely not a fairytale," she shot back, earning a low chuckle from Blake.

The nickname I'd used for her back at the truck almost slipped off my tongue again, but I caught myself. She didn't like it. There was something there that I didn't fully understand, but I was beginning to. A past she didn't want to remember, even if there was plenty of good there. Nathan had poisoned it, spreading decay through even my memories of Black Lake back in the day.

That was fine. I'd give her a new one. "Fighting words, strawberry," I whispered, low enough only she could hear. She looked up at me in surprise, and the pink in her cheeks deepened.

Perfection.

I worked to keep my wolf in check as we strode toward the long pole barn sitting back from the main drive. The earthy scent of manure and mulch filled my nostrils with the lush forest looming around us, a reminder of the wildness that ran through our veins. Wolf shifters were creatures of nature, but today, we sought answers from someone who belonged to the earth in a way even we didn't.

"Keep your senses sharp," Rowan murmured, his voice a low rumble beside me. His gaze was on me, I didn't even have to look. Alpha authority emanated from him like heat from a flame. Blake, surprisingly, didn't give a snarky response, his own eyes scanning the treeline, muscles tensed.

Rowan went first, pushing open the front door. The wood was weathered but sturdy. Despite growing up in a small town,

I hadn't spent much time around farms. I couldn't tell if this one was in good condition or if Lyra had let it slip.

A figure emerged from the back office, wiping hands on a dirt-stained apron. He looked up, the surprise at seeing guests apparent in the rise of his bushy eyebrows. His mouth worked a moment before he finally said, "How can I help you?"

It was an excellent question, considering we only had a name to go off of. Was Lyra her real name? Was she hiding here?

"We're here to see an old friend," Rowan answered smoothly.

The man in the apron took him in and cleared his throat. "Are you positive you're in the right place? I'm Carter, the manager here. We don't have many employees."

Rowan didn't flinch. "I'm not sure she is an employee. Her name's Lyra."

Carter's face immediately brightened. "Well, why didn't you say that in the first place!" He approached with a genuine smile and shook each of our hands in turn. "At first I thought you looked like trouble, but if you're Lyra's friends—" He chuckled to himself as he motioned for us to follow. "She's got connections with the strangest folk."

I frowned. "Did he just call us strange?" I whispered to Blake.

Blake nodded to Rowan. "Probably referring just to him."

Rowan shot us an annoyed glance as we trailed behind Carter, our footsteps echoing softly on the wooden floor. Rowan moved with a predator's grace, every inch the alpha leader, while Blake's presence was like a silent storm—calm until provoked. My own steps were measured, betraying nothing of my racing thoughts or the nerves that prickled beneath my skin.

The scent of soil and decay spiked as we followed Carter

into the main barn. Ghostly white fungi sprouted in deliberate rows, their caps glowing faintly in the dim light. The air was thick with moisture, a palpable presence that clung to my skin and filled my lungs.

I remembered my mother telling me how mushrooms grew. How their spores floated through the air and attached to their hosts—dead and rotting logs, mulch piles. I imagined them filling my lungs and sprouting there in my alveoli.

Rowan nudged my shoulder. "Breathe."

"I am. That's the problem."

He frowned, and I shrugged, trying to ease the tension knotting my shoulders. Rowan's presence was like the hum of electricity before a storm, impossible to ignore. With each step, my senses stretched taut, keenly attuned to the rhythm of his breath, the subtle shift of his muscles beneath his clothes.

"Careful here." Carter guided us past a low-hanging shelf laden with oyster mushrooms, their delicate frills trembling at our passing. "We try to keep the environment stable for optimal growth."

Every rustle, every drip of water from the overhead pipes, seemed amplified, yet all paled in comparison to the silent symphony that was Rowan Steele. His aura brushed against mine, unseen but as real as the weight of my own body. My wolf stirred within, restless, drawn to his strength, his certainty.

"Quite the operation you have here," Blake said.

"Thank you," Carter replied. "Mushrooms require patience and precision."

Rowan's hand brushed mine briefly as we navigated a narrow turn, sending a jolt through me that left my heart stuttering. It was an accident, surely, but my wolf seized upon the contact, craving more.

Patience and precision. That described my whole life. In my

work as an EMT I was the steady force. I was the one giving the orders and responsible for the outcomes of my patients.

To have Rowan there next to me was both terrifying and a relief so powerful it weakened my knees. *You don't have to do this alone.* My wolf pushed the thought forward, but I shook my head. I'd tried that once. I'd been a part of a pack, and where had that taken me?

But now I didn't know what all the patience and precision were for. What did I have to look forward to?

We moved deeper into the farm, the manager's voice a distant drone as he explained the intricacies of mushroom cultivation. I caught the glint of silver first—the cascade of Lyra Moonshadow's hair, stark and luminous against the earthen backdrop of the mushroom farm. It fell in a sleek river down her back as she bent over a tray of shiitake sprouts, her slender fingers working.

"Lyra," Carter called out.

She straightened, turning toward us, her violet eyes catching the dim light like the facets of a gemstone. She didn't smile.

Carter's enthusiasm wavered as he looked between her and our group. For a moment, I wondered if she was going to throw us out.

"So good to see you," Lyra replied, setting down a delicate tool on the table beside her. She wiped her hands on a cloth, every motion deliberate and unhurried. "Carter, thank you." It was a dismissal, and he understood perfectly. He gave us a final nod, then bumbled down the walkway back to the office.

"Follow me." Lyra led us away from the growing beds. We wound through narrow corridors lined with shelves heavy with fungi. The air grew cooler as we left the main pathways. Lyra pushed open a wooden door that groaned softly on its hinges, revealing a small room with shelves filled with books and strange artifacts. In the center stood a sturdy desk covered with papers and jars of peculiar herbs.

"Sit." She gestured toward a pair of mismatched chairs before perching herself on the edge of the desk, those violet eyes never leaving our faces. "I smelled you before you left the office. Impressive, considering I was surrounded by dung."

My wolf's hackles raised, and I put a hand on her muzzle. Blake and I sat obediently, but Rowan stayed standing.

"Must've been a reprieve. To smell something other than shit." Rowan put a protective hand on the back of my chair.

The corner of Lyra's mouth lifted. "Don't get your panties in a twist. It's a hobby of mine to poke alpha's with a stick."

Blake coughed next to me, covering a laugh.

Lyra folded her arms in front of her. "So. Please. Enlighten me as to why you decided to meet with the wicked witch."

Rowan glanced down at me, and I reached for my back-pack. "We found this." I pulled the dagger out and unwrapped the old shirt I'd rolled it in.

Lyra's eyes widened, the smirk leaving her face. "Ah, yes, the Relic of Binding." Lyra's fingers idly traced the wood grain of the desk. "A dangerous artifact, created to harness the power of blood, sacrifice, and the bonds we forge."

I held it out to her, but she shook her head. Rowan shifted beside me, the muscles in his jaw clenching.

Blake leaned forward, elbows on his knees. "I thought the relics were legends."

He stole the words right out of my mouth. All pups heard the stories. How there were objects forged that could bind souls and control fates. These tales were used to scare us into brushing our teeth, eating vegetables, and attending the full moon runs when the elders insisted on babbling for an hour before we could shift.

"Legends always have roots in truth." Lyra's eyes seemed to

glow. "But the relics...they are both more complex and more simple than the stories suggest."

"Simple how?" I prodded, needing to understand the force that seemed to pull at the very fibers of my being.

"Simple in its need for connection," Lyra explained. "It requires a bond, willing or not, to weave its magic. Without that, it's merely metal and intent."

"And the blood, the sacrifice?" Rowan's deep voice resonated within the close walls.

"Those are the keys to unlocking its full potential," Lyra continued, her expression unreadable. "To wield it is to accept a burden—one that should not be taken lightly."

I felt the chill of realization seep into my bones. The dagger bound us, yes, but it was the intertwining of our lives, our choices, that would determine its true power. *Had it already been used for blood?*

I thought back to the legends. About the dark witch who was said to have created the relics in the first place. "Is the rest of the story true, then?"

Lyra's gaze flickered from me to Rowan and then to Blake before she nodded slowly. "Centuries ago, there lived a dark witch named Seraphina. She was powerful and feared, but not without her enemies." Her voice was soft, almost reverent. "To protect herself and to cement her power, she created five objects, each imbued with a fraction of her essence."

"Five?" Rowan's question echoed my own. The stories all differed in how many relics there were. Some told of a statue hidden deep in the forest or an ancient book buried in the earth.

"Few know the full extent of her legacy," Lyra replied. "The dagger is but one. There are four others, scattered across the world, lost to time and greed."

As she spoke, her hands moved with purpose and grace—a

fluidity that betrayed something otherworldly beneath her human facade. She looked the part. Her clothes. Her hair held back with a bandana. It reminded me of myself, how I'd learned to blend into the human world, to hide the primal nature that lurked beneath my skin. As an EMT, I'd mastered the art of maintaining control, of keeping my wolf at bay even when every instinct screamed otherwise.

But there was something in Lyra's demeanor that didn't quite fit, a sense of belonging perpetually out of reach. We could walk among them and talk like them, but we would never truly be *one* of them. Our very beings were etched with the indelible mark of magic and moonlight, our souls inter-twined with forces beyond the mundane.

"Seraphina's creations. They're meant to be together?" Blake asked, drawing me back to the conversation.

"Perhaps," Lyra said, her eyes narrowing slightly. "Or perhaps they are meant to stay hidden. Together, they hold a power that no single being should wield. Separately, they are dangerous enough."

"Like calls to like," I murmured, the strange coolness still seeping through the fabric between my hand and the metal. The silver blade caught the light.

"Unfortunately, yes." Lyra pushed off the desk. She glanced at the blade warily, then pushed her hands into the pockets of her faded jeans. "How did you come by this?"

I quickly rolled the shirt around the dagger and shoved it back into my backpack, debating whether I should tell the truth. Lyra was a witch, and while the elders seemed to be frightened of her, she had allowed us into her personal space. She'd answered our questions. I figured I could show the same trust. "A friend of mine went missing. I found this hidden in her things."

Lyra raised an eyebrow. "She left it behind."

"I don't think she left willingly."

The witch nodded, pulling her silver hair over her shoulder. "Those who touch the blade aren't often convinced to part with it."

Convinced. The word sent a shiver down my spine. "Does it already...has it already been used to bind?"

Lyra's violet eyes darkened. "That blade is older than your magic." She glanced down at my bag. "Pray you never hear the words it whispers." She pulled one of the jars off the desk, inspected it, and handed it to Rowan. "Something you might want to keep close, alpha."

Rowan

Someone was seeking relics? Relics existed? How the hell hadn't I been aware of that? How had one been sitting a few kilometers from us? My wolf growled at the thought of it. Protecting my pack was more than an obligation. It was the very essence of my being, the drumbeat to which my heart synchronized.

With every step I took through the underbrush, the coil of anticipation tightened within me. My muscles thrummed with restless energy, the kind that only came when the stakes were this high. Betrayal had once torn through our ranks like wildfire, leaving scars that ached at the mere thought of history repeating itself. I couldn't—wouldn't—let that happen again.

I jumped to the lower branch of a cedar and pressed my boots against the trunk, then monkeyed my way up into the branches until I had a clear view of Evelyn's hotel room across the street. I wasn't going to sit outside her door again after the look she'd given me, but I sure as hell wasn't going to leave her defenseless.

Rowan. Jasper's voice cut through the mental fog. I wasn't in my wolf form, and I knew how much effort that took. *We've got patrols covered. Stay where you are. We trust you.*

After Blake dropped me off at my truck, I'd gone back to the garage and talked with Jasper there. I was supposed to be working. More than that, I was supposed to be fulfilling our obligations with Tori and Mara.

But while Jasper hadn't mated, he knew the storm roiling inside me. His words were a balm, a reminder that I wasn't alone in this fight. As my second-in-command, he was more than just a loyal wolf. He was the backbone of our pack when uncertainty loomed overhead. With him holding down the fort, I could chase the elusive threads of this mystery and protect my mate without fear for the safety of those I held dear.

Theoretically. It was never going to be possible for me to sit back and relax.

I'm here, I projected back, my mind's voice as firm as the set of my jaw. *Thank you.*

I don't mess around, Jasper replied, the mental equivalent of his usual curt nod. I chuckled, shifting in the tree until my back rested against the trunk. I rubbed my sap-smeared palms on my jeans and drew a deep breath.

I would stay here all night if I had to. I'd never needed as much sleep as other wolves, and since becoming alpha, that disparity had only grown. It was convenient on nights like this. Less convenient when I was pacing around my empty house in the middle of the night.

My heart picked up speed at the thought of Evelyn standing in my living room. Of her sharing my bed. I stared hard enough at her door, I wondered if it might spontaneously combust. Was she undressing? Showering? Pulling her hair up and—

I jolted so hard, I nearly lost my seat. Evelyn's door was opening. I gripped the branch above me and leaned forward, then cursed under my breath. *That little minx.*

Evelyn was dressed in all black, carrying her backpack. She closed the door and walked to the stairs with her head down.

"Damn it, Strawberry." I launched myself out of the tree, the bark scraping my neck and arms as I crashed to the ground. What the hell was she thinking?

I blew out a breath. I knew what she was thinking. She was a tracker, and she'd obviously kept to herself some of the clues she'd gathered. My wolf groaned at the thought. I wanted her to share things with me. To let me protect her. If anything happened to her...

I broke into a run. She was already crossing the street and I was a block behind her. With every step, my senses stretched out like tendrils, seeking her scent.

I moved silently, my boots pressing into the soft forest floor, until her sweet scent filled my nostrils. I hesitated. She hadn't told me she was leaving. I doubted she'd be happy to find me following her.

I wanted to call out, to demand answers like I did from my pack. But I wasn't Evelyn's alpha. Not yet. There was more to this than met the eye, and if there was one thing I'd learned as an alpha, it was that patience often revealed more than rash action ever could.

Easier said than done.

So, I followed, keeping my presence a secret. The distance

between us remained constant, her figure visible between the trees ahead of me. But when I glanced once at the rising gibbous moon, I lost her. My wolf pressed so hard against my senses, I nearly cried out.

I abandoned all pretense of stealth and bolted, my head whipping from side to side. Tracking Evelyn should have been easy—my senses were honed for this—but she was no ordinary wolf.

"Following me, Rowan?" Her voice cut through the silence, an accusatory lilt to her words.

I skidded to a stop in the leaves, relief flooding through me. When I could finally draw a full breath, I turned to face her. "Just out for a run."

Evelyn took a step toward me. Her hair was tucked in her hood, her hands wrapped around the straps of her backpack. "You're a terrible liar."

A grin tugged at the corner of my lips despite my wolf still pacing restlessly. He was pissed. I should've been pissed. But standing in front of her, I knew that was never going to be a possibility. "You look good."

Evelyn rolled her eyes. "That's what you're saying to me right now? Not 'I'm sorry, Evelyn, I realize you're a grown-ass wolf, and you don't need a chaperone?'" She leaned against a tree, arms crossed over her chest, one brow arched in challenge.

"I realize you're a grown-ass wolf."

"What about the apology?"

My jaw worked. "You said I was a terrible liar."

Evelyn pursed her lips. "You are..."

"Incredible."

She scoffed, pushing off the tree.

"So hot you want to put down your bag and come back to my place." I grinned as I fell into step next to her.

"In your dreams."

"Literally." The clock was ticking. I wasn't going to pretend I felt less than I did.

Evelyn shot me a look and walked faster.

"So where are we headed?" I trailed her like a pup. She didn't answer but also didn't tell me to get the hell out of Dodge, so I figured that was best case scenario.

We moved in unison through the dark tapestry of the woods. When she slowed, I slowed. My curiosity itched at the back of my throat, but I kept my mouth shut. I was there next to her. It didn't matter where we ended up.

The scent of damp earth and decaying leaves mingled with the faint smell of wood smoke as we neared the edge of the clearing. That's when I saw it. A low cabin nestled against the hill. I growled low in my throat, and Evelyn held up a finger. Every instinct screamed caution, every rustle of the trees a potential threat. We were wolves in enemy territory, and the pounding of my heart matched the thrum of danger in the air.

I moved closer, pressing my shoulder against hers. *What is this place?* I sent to her head.

Evelyn's eyes widened. I watched her trying to answer the same way I'd asked, then finally gave a frustrated huff and leaned in. "This is a cabin."

I breathed a laugh. "No shit."

Her lips twitched. "I caught Callista's scent at the pack meeting on Justin. Then I caught it again when we were leaving the parking lot. I wondered if there was something in the woods, and there was."

"It's here?"

She nodded. "Window on the left looks open."

"No, Ev—"

She was already moving.

I bolted after her, staying glued to her flank. There were no lights on. No vehicle in the drive. That didn't mean anything with shifters. I scanned the ground, looking for fresh footprints.

A rustle to our right froze us both, our bodies instinctively crouching low against the wet earth. The forest had been eerily silent around the house, a silence that now shattered with the subtle snap of a twig under careful weight. My wolf senses prickled with an awareness that tightened my muscles, ready for anything.

"Scouts," Evelyn breathed out, her voice barely a sound in the still night. "Kitimat."

The truth of it sank into my bones. I hadn't been paying attention to how far we'd traveled. How had I not recognized when we'd passed over the Kitimat boundary?

It was one thing to risk a stealthy break-in. It was another to do so with the enemy lurking just within striking distance. "Whose house is this?" I mouthed.

Evelyn dropped her eyes, and I had my answer. I wanted to grab her by the shoulders and shake her. She was coming to Nathan's cabin alone? I didn't give a shit if he was still rumored to be up north, he was an alpha. Justin had nearly gone for her throat at the meeting, and out here? There would be nothing to stop him.

"Stay down," I commanded, though I knew there was no need. Evelyn understood the stakes as well as I did, her body already pressed to the ground, her athletic form blending seamlessly with the night.

My eyes never left the dark outline of the trees where the noise had come from, my ears straining for any other giveaway signs. A flicker of movement, a whisper of displaced air—anything that would give away their position. But the scouts were good, trained to move unseen, unheard.

Evelyn's nostrils flared as she closed her eyes, inhaling deeply. "She was inside, Rowan. I have to go in."

My heart sped in my chest. No, my wolf barked. He was right. This was stupidity at its finest. But as her hazel eyes gazed up at me, I couldn't put my paw down.

I put out my hands in a stirrup. "Give me your damn foot."

SEVENTEEN

Evelyn

The window track scraped my stomach as I dropped onto Nathan's leather couch. This place—I knew it. Nathan spoke of it once. A hidden sanctuary, he'd called it. His man cave. Deep in pack lands where an alpha could retreat.

I scoffed internally. I could only imagine what he got up to here away from prying eyes. A shiver wracked my body as I righted myself. The entire place reeked of him. My wolf shrank back, cowering within me. *She remembered, too.* Remembered his cold eyes and cruel touch, the way he crushed us under his thumb.

Memories flooded my head. The coppery tang of blood in my mouth as I bit my cheek to keep from screaming. Sinking to the plush rug, fighting to breathe through the panic squeezing my lungs.

My hands started to shake. What if coming here was a mistake? What if he was here? What if—

I gasped as a hand settled on my shoulder, flinching on instinct before Rowan's scent wrapped around me like a blanket. I leaned back into his chest without thinking and felt his twitch of surprise.

"I'm sorry." I said the words, but couldn't pull away. The steady beat of his heart echoed through me, drawing my pulse away from panic.

Rowan slipped his arm protectively across my chest, and I clung to it. "Don't be." After a few long seconds, he let go to rise and close the window, locking it and drawing the shade. "We don't have to do this," he murmured, blue eyes searching mine with concern. "Say the word, and we leave. Right now."

I pressed my lips together and shook my head. Callista's scent was here. Hard to find because of so much Nathan, but it was stronger here than in the woods.

I blinked as my eyes adjusted, trying to reconcile the decrepit outside with the lavish furnishings within. Expensive leather couches, gleaming hardwood floors, tasteful artwork on the walls. It was like stepping into an alternate reality.

Rowan ground his teeth.

"We have to check the rooms."

Rowan's face hardened. He turned to face me. "Fine. But we do this my way now, Strawberry."

Warmth spread through my middle at the sound of that name on his lips. It was silly. I'd mocked Bruce endlessly at work when I found out he'd been calling some girl *muffin*. But the way it sounded from him...well. I might've felt a tad less judgy.

Rowan slipped the straps of my bag off my back and slung it over his shoulder, and I could see the resolve in his eyes. He'd given all he could, and if I pushed him on this, he would break.

"Your way," I whispered, and his eyes melted like mountain pools.

Rowan pulled me close, folding me into him like a hen with her chick. We moved from room to room with Rowan keeping me in his vision at all times as he cleared closets and bathrooms. We found no trace of Callista. No clothing. No toothbrushes.

Her scent permeated the air in the kitchen but then vanished. A dead end.

Helpless rage built in my chest, bubbling up my throat. I slammed my fist into the kitchen doorframe. "He has her, Rowan! That bastard has my best friend, and it's all my fault!"

Strong arms wrapped around me from behind, pulling me against a broad chest. "We'll find her. I swear it." Rowan's voice rumbled through me. "But how in the hell could you think this was your fault?"

A broken sob escaped me. "You don't understand. The things he did..." I shuddered violently. "I should have stopped him. Should have been stronger—"

Rowan spun me to face him, eyes blazing. "You listen to me, Evelyn Berry. Nathan's actions are on him and him alone. You survived. You escaped. That was miraculous, do you hear me?"

I nodded, tears streaming down my cheeks. "But—"

"No." He shook his head. "Nathan's an alpha. Whether he got there rightfully or not, his pack is his responsibility. You and Callie were his responsibility and he treated you like shit." Rowan's eyes drank in the shadows from every corner of the room. "He'll pay. That's a promise."

I nodded and sniffled as his hands cupped my face tenderly. "It kills me that that's what you thought love was."

I exhaled, wrapping my hands over his. "I never thought that was love. I just..."

Rowan fixed his eyes on me, his wolf so close to the surface his eyes gleamed. My wolf rose to meet him, and energy pulsed between us.

"You never thought you were worthy of it." Rowan's voice rumbled through the kitchen, sinking into me like a hand against soft clay.

"We're going to rewrite this story. Give it a new ending."

"Rowan—"

Without another word, he scooped me up and strode purposefully toward the bedroom. My heart hammered wildly, but I didn't resist, some part of me understanding his intent. Needing it.

Gently, so gently, Rowan lay me on the bed, settling beside me. One hand smoothed my hair back as the other found my hip, his thumb caressing soothing circles.

"You are worthy of worship," he murmured. "Can I show you?"

I swallowed hard, nerves and longing warring within. "I...I'm afraid," I confessed.

"Of me?"

I shook my head. "No." It was the truth. Maybe I had been afraid of him, but the relief of his scent moments ago spoke truth. *No.* I wasn't afraid of Rowan Steele.

Words bubbled up my throat before I could stop them. "I'm afraid of wanting too much. Of losing myself again."

Rowan's lips brushed my forehead. "You won't ever lose yourself. Because I'll be there to catch you."

His hands found mine, then slid up to cover my wrists. With aching tenderness, he lifted them from the bed, stretching my arms over my head. "I'm going to show you what love looks like. What you're worthy of."

My pulse fluttered wildly in my throat, my wolf panting in anticipation. Somewhere far in the distance I was aware that we were still in Nathan's cabin. That we'd come here searching for Callista, and that the dagger was still wrapped up in my bag on the floor next to the bed.

But all thoughts left my head as Rowan's breath warmed the inside of my elbow. Holy shit. He kissed me with such tenderness, my stomach dropped out from under me. Rowan trailed his lips up to my wrist and back again, then threw his leg over my hips, crouching over me as he replicated his soft torture on my second side.

"I love the scent of you," He murmured into the soft flesh beneath my shirt sleeve. "Your skin is like velvet."

Tears stung the corners of my eyes. Nathan had never said anything like that to me. He hated my arms—said they looked weak. As if reading my thoughts, a low growl rumbled in Rowan's chest. "Terrible liar, remember?"

A ragged laugh escaped my lips, and Rowan drank up the sound like it was water. He dropped his hands from my wrists and traced my edges, making me shiver. His fingers landed at the hem of my shirt. "Is this okay?"

I nodded, then sank into the bed as his palms pressed flat over my stomach. He moved down the bed and lifted the fabric, pressing his cheek over my belly button.

I pulled my hands down from over my head and threaded my fingers in his hair, trailing over the tops of his ears and lightly scratching his scalp. I loved how his stubble felt against my skin. Loved how I could hear his breath coming faster. And his scent—the wild spice of his arousal sent my wolf into a near frenzy.

"Rowan—"

"Shh. My way."

I grinned. "That was regarding the room search."

"I don't remember putting any time limitations on that edict." He trailed his fingers over my ribs, then lifted his head to look at me as his hands found the waistband of my pants. "This okay?"

My breath caught in my throat. I shouldn't be doing this. I shouldn't be giving in to this magnetic pull. I was only in Black Lake for a few more days, and both of us knew it. Yet I couldn't stop myself from nodding.

Rowan didn't drop his eyes as he flicked the button open and pulled down on the zipper. His chest rose and fell as he pulled the waistband down over my hips.

Finally, he let himself look. I shifted on the bed and lifted my legs to allow him to pull my pants free. He tossed them on the floor, his eyes traveling over my bare legs. I was instantly grateful I'd worn nice underwear. It wasn't sexy, but at least it was new. Ish.

"Any man who took you for granted is a damn fool." He lifted my right leg and ducked underneath it, resting my knee on his shoulder.

My wolf practically salivated seeing him there between my thighs, and my head spun like a top. I had no idea what he was going to do next, and the possibilities both thrilled and terrified me. *Trust him.*

I wanted to. I wanted to give myself over to him so much it physically ached. But Nathan had been kind once, too. He'd lavished me with gifts and praise for months before the first time he hit me. Was that what alpha's did? Lulled you into a sense of security before they took everything they wanted?

A desire to please him flooded me, making me desperate to keep this feeling—to keep him interested so this would never end. I put my hand out, feeling for his belt, but Rowan circled his hand over mine.

"No, Strawberry. You don't need to lift a finger." He placed my palm on the bed. I couldn't keep the fear from flickering across my face, and Rowan read me like a book. "There is nothing you could do or neglect to do that would make me walk away right now. Do you understand?"

I bit the inside of my cheek, and Rowan slid closer, draping my leg over his back. "You deserve this. You deserve to lie back and close your eyes and be touched. Be kissed. You don't have to earn this, Evelyn."

A tear slipped from the corner of my eye and rolled down my cheek. Rowan reached out and swiped it away with his thumb, then pressed it to his tongue.

"I want to believe you." My voice was barely a whisper.

He nodded and turned his head, pressing his mouth against the inside of my knee. "Wanting to believe is enough." His eyelids shuttered closed as he wrapped his hand around my thigh, rolling his tongue slowly over my skin.

Rowan took his time kissing every part of me. Almost. He never flirted with the lines of my underwear, even when I was desperate for him to try. When he finished, after flipping me onto my stomach and rubbing every muscle in my back, he lay down next to me, pulling me against him.

For long moments, we simply lay entwined, Rowan's hands skimming up and down my arm in gentle strokes. My core felt like it was filled with hot coals, but all the tension had seeped from my limbs, and I breathed deeper than I had in years.

"Tell me a story," I whispered into the silence. "Something happy."

Rowan hummed thoughtfully, the sound rumbling against my shoulder blades. "Remember that summer before..." He trailed off, and I knew he meant before everything fell apart, before the pack splintered.

"It's okay." I ran my fingers over his. It was. Somehow hearing Rowan talk about my past didn't seem nearly as scary as it had the first time that topic had been broached.

He cleared his throat. "We found that hidden swimming hole in the woods."

A smile tugged at my lips, the memory rising hazy and golden. "I remember. You dared me to jump from the top of the waterfall."

"And you did." Pride warmed his tone. "Fearless, even then. I think—" He exhaled, and I squeezed his hand.

"You think what?"

"Maybe my wolf knew something even then."

My breath caught as Rowan's arms tightened around me.

"I know this isn't the time or place," he whispered. "But I need you to know, Evelyn...how I feel won't change. I won't ever force you to accept this. But I'm not going to stop trying."

Tears pricked my eyes, emotions too tangled to name rising in my throat.

Rowan shifted, tugging me until I rolled over on my back, then cupped my face, tilting it up until our gazes locked. "No expectations. No alpha demands. I just want you to know that you're loved. Unconditionally. Irrevocably."

A sob hitched in my chest. I pressed my face into his neck, letting his heartbeat anchor me. "I don't know what to say," I rasped.

And for the first time in longer than I could remember, I felt exactly what he'd set out to do. The first sentences of a new story.

One where I was cherished.

Treasured.

Safe.

Rowan held me until my breathing settled, then pulled back to look at me. "I do have one request, though."

I raised an eyebrow and flicked my gaze down to his hips. He laughed and shook his head. "I know you're curious, but you're going to have to wait." I smacked his chest, and he held onto my hand. "As much as I love sleeping on concrete or tree branches—"

"You *were* sleeping outside my room!"

His grin widened. "I think you should stay with Will and Marissa."

I frowned. "I'm not going to be a charity case."

"It's not charity. Actually, it's a favor. Marissa's within a month of delivery. I'd love to know someone else was watching out for her."

"And…"

"They live down the street from me, so I can keep an eye on you."

"There it is."

He pressed his lips against my forehead. "I'm going to do it either way. This option gives you home-cooked meals and better carpet."

"When you say it like that, how can a girl refuse?"

Relief eased the tension in Rowan's broad shoulders. "Thank you. You have no idea what this means to me."

I managed a smile, but it felt brittle. Trepidation still churned in my gut.

Trust him.

Rowan rose and found my clothes. I thanked him, and then as I dressed, I ignored the warning bells clanging in my head. I pushed aside the reminders that I was heading back to Seattle, that it wasn't safe for me to be here. Mostly, I prayed that by letting Rowan in, I wasn't making the same mistake over again.

CHAPTER

EIGHTEEN

With Evelyn standing on the step next to me, I rapped my knuckles against the solid wood of the front door. It swung open almost immediately, revealing Will, his warm smile welcoming us in. Beside him stood his wife, Marissa, cradling her swollen belly with a gentleness that spoke volumes of the precious life growing within her.

"Rowan," Will greeted me, clasping my forearm in a firm grip.

"Marissa." I nodded toward her. Normally, I'd hug her, too, but with Will on edge, I didn't want to give him something to grumble about. I'd spoken with him through the pack bond on the way over. He was nervous to have someone staying with them, and I understood that.

I promised I would be watching closely. We only had a few pregnant she-wolves, and each one was a treasure to be cherished and protected.

Truthfully, it was a compromise to have Evelyn even a few doors down from me. I wanted her next to me at all times. In my bed where I could watch over her. But based on the emotions that poured out of her at the cabin, I knew she was fragile. I didn't want to push any more than I had to.

Will, understandably, didn't want the dagger anywhere close to his pregnant mate. It took a little cajoling, but Evelyn had finally agreed to let me store it at my house until we could figure out what to do next.

"Come in, please," Marissa stepped aside, her smile softening the sharp lines of my worry. She moved with an ease that belied her condition, but Will hovered near her, ready to offer support or punch someone's throat at a moment's notice.

"Are you feeling well?" I couldn't help asking, my eyes scanning her for any sign of discomfort. "Is there anything you need?"

"Nothing more than your company, Alpha Rowan," she replied with a lightness that eased the tension coiling in my shoulders. "We're doing just fine, aren't we, love?"

"Never better." Will wrapped an arm around her shoulders.

I led Evelyn into the heart of Will's living room, my hand at the small of her back—a silent promise that I was there, that she was not alone in this unfamiliar territory.

"Will, Marissa," I started, my voice gruff with barely-contained urgency, "Evelyn will be staying with you for a while." The weight of my responsibility as alpha pressed down on me, and I fought to keep my tone even. "Her protection is paramount."

Will's gaze met mine, steady and understanding. "We'll

guard her as if she were our own," he said, a solemn vow from one who understood the depth of my commitment.

Marissa stepped forward, her eyes soft but fierce. "No harm will come to her here, Rowan."

"Thank you," I murmured, my relief a palpable thing as I saw the resolve in their eyes. I trusted them implicitly, but leaving Evelyn in someone else's care didn't sit well with me.

"Rowan," Will's voice pulled me back from my thoughts, "there's been talk—rumors of unrest stirring in the neighboring packs. Shifters moving through territories uninvited, challenging the old ways."

I tensed, instincts flaring to life. "How recent are these movements?"

"Last few nights. Can't say if it's rogue wolves or something more coordinated."

"More coordinated?" Marissa echoed, a frown creasing her brow. "Do you think they're planning something?"

"Maybe," I admitted, my mind racing through possibilities and threats. "It could be a power play, a prelude to a challenge. Or worse."

"An uprising?" Will suggested, his voice low.

"Could be," I said grimly. "Which means we need to be prepared. We can't let anything threaten our pack—or any of the others."

Will nodded grimly. "Sounds like you have work to do."

I looked back at Evelyn. She gave a small smile and nodded. It felt like tearing my heart from my chest to turn my back and walk to the porch, but I forced my legs to move. There was much to do, many miles to cover before I could rest.

My boots crunched softly over the needle-strewn path, the moon a slender crescent in the night sky, illuminating the way to the rendezvous point. Jasper and Lana might already be waiting.

After what felt like both a snap of my fingers and an eternity, I arrived at our meeting spot—a small clearing guarded by towering redwoods. A fallen log served as a makeshift bench, its surface smoothed by countless seasons. Here, beneath the watchful gaze of ancient trees, decisions that shaped the fate of our pack had been made. Tonight would be no different.

I perched on the log. Jasper and Lana were never late, yet every second stretched, taut as a bowstring. I flexed my fingers, my wolf pacing restlessly within.

Finally, I lifted my head, nostrils flaring as I scented them before they broke through the foliage. They emerged like specters from the dark, their forms slipping silently into the moonlit clearing. "Rowan," Jasper's voice was a low rumble, his mercenary-like build cutting an imposing silhouette.

"Jasper. Lana." My gaze flicked to her, the sarcasm that usually danced in her eyes replaced with solemnity. Their expressions mirrored the gravity I felt clawing at my insides.

Lana exhaled. "We've patrolled the borders. No signs of immediate threat, but I don't like the energy."

I nodded. "And you both? How are you holding up?"

"Ready to tear into anyone who threatens us." Lana brushed back her long dark hair. "We're solid, Rowan. But what about Evelyn? Is she safe?"

"Will and his wife have her under their protection."

"How'd you convince her to leave that shithole of a hotel?" Jasper asked.

"Magicians don't reveal their secrets."

Lana turned to Jasper. "Earrings?"

He shook his head. "Nah. Probably oral."

Lana rolled her eyes.

"Jasper, report," I barked, pretending I hadn't heard either of them.

He smirked. "Tori's got us on the eastern ridge for the next twenty-four hours."

"Perfect. I'll join you for the aerial sweep." I ran a hand through my hair. "I don't have enough information, but someone's hunting the relics."

Jasper frowned. "Relics? As in from the stories?"

"Exactly." I leaned over my knees. "Evelyn is tracking the trail, but so far we only have dead ends."

Lana nodded, then paused. When she spoke, her voice was low. "Rowan...Kitimat is expecting their alpha as early as tomorrow night."

My chest tightened. "He won't cross territory lines."

"And if he does?" Jasper raised an eyebrow.

My wolf let out a low growl. "Then we'll be ready."

CHAPTER
NINETEEN

I stared at the front door, shifting my weight on my feet. A community picnic. *Why the hell was I considering going to a community picnic?* My friend was missing, and I only had three days to find her, and yet there I was wearing my favorite jeans and a tank top, holding a bowl of freshly cut watermelon.

My phone buzzed, jarring me from my thoughts. I set the bowl down on the side table and pulled it from my back pocket.

BRUCE:

> Hope you're enjoying your little retreat while
> I'm drowning in paperwork here. Remember
> the Fairclough case? Yeah, that's on you.

Bastard. I typed back swiftly, my fingers a staccato rhythm on the screen.

> Enjoy the mountain of files, Bruce. Consider it payback for all those coffees you 'forgot' to pay for

I swiped back to my messages, realizing that was the first text I'd received since taking off at the beginning of the week. That was pathetic. Also not exactly a surprise, and I already regretted giving Bruce my personal number.

"Hey, you good?" Marissa asked behind me.

I turned, slipping my phone back in my pocket. "Yeah." I picked up the bowl of watermelon, my thoughts spinning as Marissa walked to the door and slipped on her flip-flops. I didn't have another lead. I wanted something to do—some other clue that would lead me back to Callista's trail, but I had nothing. Going out into the community would give me a better chance of finding something than sitting here in Will and Marissa's house.

"Ready?"

I nodded, then followed Marissa out the door.

We made our way toward the communal space where the lunch was held, guided by the sound of laughter and the welcoming aroma of home-cooked food. Not the scent I should be following, but who was I kidding. Smoked meat? Yes, please.

The clearing was abuzz with activity. Pack members and humans mingled. Children darted between tables, their giggles punctuating the hum of conversation as they played tag around, under, and between their parents.

I paused at the fringe of the gathering, taking in the festoon of colors from tablecloths fluttering in the gentle breeze, the array of dishes. Smoked salmon, wild berry preserves, and freshly baked breads seemed to call out *this is what you've been missing!*

It was true. In Seattle I went from work to home, wash, rinse, repeat. If there were events like this, I definitely didn't know about them.

"Hey, Evelyn! Over here!" The call came from a cluster of Black Lake Pack members lounging on checkered blankets. Why were they being so nice to me? Some of them had to still remember who I was. If not them, then their parents. Wouldn't they want to get as far from me as possible?

"Didn't think you'd miss out on Marianne's blackberry pie, eh?" teased a burly man with a grin that crinkled the corners of his eyes. His laughter was infectious.

"Wouldn't dream of it." I mustered as much cheerfulness as I could manage. The group parted to make room for me, and I settled onto the soft grass and set down my bowl of watermelon. A group of three toddlers instantly stuffed their hands in for a piece.

"Bacon-wrapped date?" A woman whose silver hair spoke of wisdom and years spent nurturing the bond between shifter and human passed me a plate.

A man wearing a Nanaimo EMT hat passed me a plate piled high with home-cooked rolls.

"You're EMT?" I asked, knowing there was a chance he got the hat at a Value Village or something.

He nodded. "Thirty years."

"You work around here?"

"For Kooteney Health. Three days a week. You?"

I shook my head. "I was with a group in Seattle." I blinked. *Was.* Why had I said was? "Sorry, I am with a group in Seattle. Heading back in a few days."

Laughter erupted from a nearby table where children were engaged in a spirited debate over who would win in a race—a wolf or a deer. I grinned, thinking one of us should shift and show them.

I caught sight of Rowan across the square. He was flipping burgers, but his eyes flicked to mine the second I looked in his direction. "I think I'll go make up a plate." I excused myself and started toward him.

"Having fun?" He asked as I approached.

I nodded, shoving my hands in the back pockets of my jeans. "I don't know how you look so relaxed."

He shrugged. "I can be worried about my pack and enjoy an afternoon in the sun. Both can be true." Rowan nodded to the table next to him, and I grabbed a plate. I didn't have much of an appetite, but I took some pasta salad and veggies and dip. Rowan insisted on making me a burger.

I sat at the table next to where he was working and chatted with him while he finished cooking up the last sleeve of patties. As he was untying his apron, one of the Black Lake elders approached. He didn't have to announce his station. If I couldn't already sense his energy and standing, the way Rowan straightened would've given it away.

He looked between the two of us, his eyes narrowing.

Rowan grabbed him a plate. "Have you had a burger yet, Elder Kurt?"

I dipped a carrot in ranch and watched as Rowan helped him with his plate. The elders weren't incapable of taking care of themselves, but most of them had lived for hundreds of years. It was an act of gratitude and respect to serve them.

"What was that all about?" I asked as Elder Kurt made his way back to his group.

Rowan shrugged, and I raised an eyebrow. He sat across from me, and I couldn't help but notice how his t-shirt stretched over his shoulders as he leaned over the table. "They have opinions."

I frowned. "About what?"

"About me."

"As alpha?"

He picked up a tab from a can of pop sitting on the table and flicked it between his fingers. All I could think about was how those fingers had been all over me the night before. "More about the next blood moon."

Realization hit. "Ah. They want you to mate."

"Apparently, I'm ancient."

I reached out and ran my finger over the streak of grey in his stubble. "Proof."

He grinned and reached up for my hand. "I'm glad you came today."

Laughter bubbled up from a group engaged in a game of horseshoes.

"Rowan! Show us how it's done!" a burly man called, waving a horseshoe in the air with a wink.

"Want to play?" Rowan's eyes sparkled.

I threw my plate in the garbage and followed him over to the pits. Despite the undercurrent of mystery tugging at my thoughts, I let the competitive spirit of the moment sweep me along. We made a couple of practice throws, but when Rowan got one centered on the post, I knew it was game time.

The cold iron felt grounding in my hands, a tangible reminder that not everything had to be about the weight of duty. I focused, aimed, and with a swift flick of my wrist, sent the horseshoe sailing toward the stake.

It landed with a satisfying clink, encircling the metal post perfectly. Cheers erupted around me, and my lips curved into a triumphant smile.

"You didn't tell us she was a ringer." The man who'd invited us over nudged my shoulder, then flinched and moved back a few steps. His eyes flicked between me and Rowan.

Oh geez. I turned to Rowan and pursed my lips.

"What?" He didn't look the least bit apologetic as he wound up for another throw. "He shouldn't have touched you."

We played a few more rounds, and for those few hours, the search for Callista and the missing dagger was a distant thought. The sun was sinking behind the towering redwoods, painting the sky in hues of lavender as I helped with cleanup.

"Does the pack sponsor things like this?" I asked Will as he held a trash bag for me to scoop up plates left on one of the picnic tables.

He nodded. "Rowan thinks it's important to foster good relationships with the community."

I agreed. That was something I always wished we did in Kitimat. Up there it was us verses them. Full stop.

Rowan was waiting for me on the sidewalk. He put out his arm, and I looped mine in his as we walked the few blocks home. "Want to see my house?" he asked.

"Is that your best line?"

He laughed. "I don't know, you tell me."

"Terrible."

"How about, 'Hey Evelyn, want to come over to strategize?'"

I grinned. "Much better." He led me past Will and Marissa's, and truth be told, I was impressed. Based on how awake my wolf was anytime Rowan was near, I knew his wolf must be clamoring for us to solidify our mating bond. He was an alpha, and yet I didn't see him commanding anyone in his pack to bend to his will. It was like...they wanted to follow him. A foreign concept for me.

Rowan dropped my arm and walked up the steps, then took out his key and unlocked the door. He flicked on the lights, and I followed him in. It was a modern rambler, and I immediately loved his taste. Simple leather furniture, a brick fireplace on the far wall. "You have curtains? I thought bachelors weren't supposed to know about window treatments."

"That's what Lana's for." Rowan set the keys on the island in the kitchen and opened the fridge. "Seltzer?"

I nodded and took a seat on the bar stool. He opened the can for me and set it on the counter.

"Can I see the dagger again?" I asked. I doubted I would notice anything new, but it was currently our only lead.

Rowan nodded and disappeared into the hall. A moment later, his footsteps came quick. The moment I saw his face, a chill settled in my bones.

Rowan raked his hand through his hair, stalking into the kitchen. "Evelyn, I'm so sorry. I put it in a hidden drawer in the back of my closet. I don't know..."

Blood rushed in my ears, drowning him out. The dagger, the one thing anchoring me to my mission, the one lead I had in finding Callista, was gone.

CHAPTER

TWENTY

Rowan

one. The word hit me with the force of a charging bull. I'd convinced Evelyn to trust me with it—I'd told her she could trust me. How could it be gone?

Evelyn followed me into my bedroom, and I watched from the door as she surveyed the space. She closed her eyes, and my wolf stood at attention as I sensed hers working to the surface.

"Do you smell that?" Evelyn asked.

I drew a breath. I didn't sense anything out of the ordinary, but maybe that was because I was used to the smells of my pack. If Evelyn found something—if she linked it to one of the members of my pack—

She met my stare head-on, her eyes fierce and unwavering. "That scent. It doesn't belong to Black Lake. It's... different. Strange. And it's intentionally covered, like someone's trying to mask their trail from us."

131

"Masked?" My senses were sharp, honed by years of leading my pack, yet this scent eluded me completely. A cold finger trailed down my spine, awakening a primal unease. "Why can't I smell it?"

"Whoever it is, they're clever. They've managed to conceal their scent, but not completely. There's a trace, something synthetic maybe, that I can follow." She rushed out of the room.

"Where are you going?"

"To get my backpack and med kit!" She threw on her shoes and ran down the steps.

"Evelyn!" I raced after her, and when I arrived at Will's, she was already throwing her backpack over her shoulder.

"C'mon." She led me back to my house, walked down the hall, took another moment in the room, then raced out the back door.

I launched out after her and nearly bowled her over.

"Ow, Rowan!" She grabbed onto my arms to keep from falling backward onto the deck.

"Why'd you stop?"

Evelyn tilted her head up and met my eyes. "I was waiting for you."

I stood there, the weight of her admission anchoring me to the spot. Just yesterday, she'd been sneaking out of a hotel room, and now...My heart thundered, a wild rhythm against my ribs. This fierce, lone wolf—a beta without a pack—had chosen to lean on me. In that moment, our bond solidified, another thread snapping into place as tangible as the boards under my boots.

"Let me carry that." I pointed at the bag.

She didn't argue. We jogged down the path behind my house until we were concealed by the trees. Without hesitation, Evelyn began to strip. I turned my back and did the same, using every shred of self-control not to turn and look at her.

"You good?" I asked.

Evelyn barked in response. She'd already shifted. I turned and saw her back to me, her clothes in a neat pile on the ground. I shoved them in the bag and added mine, then zipped it. I barely had to think it before my wolf flew forward, bursting out of me.

I picked up the backpack with my mouth.

What the hell is happening? Jasper's rough voice echoed in my head.

If this is a sex thing, you need to shield your emoting, Lana added, a smirk in her mental tone.

Right. That surge of emotion from the time I chased after Evelyn to me standing on the back patio? My second and third —possibly further down the line—felt it.

Not a sex thing. We're following a lead, I growled back.

It felt too warm and fuzzy, Jasper snarked.

Evelyn nudged me with her nose. I nodded, and the forest swallowed us whole, dense foliage blurring into a sea of green and brown as we bolted forward. Evelyn led the way, her keen tracker's nose scanning the underbrush for any sign of the trail she'd found earlier. I trailed behind her, feeling like a novice rather than the alpha. It was disconcerting, being unable to smell what she could. My heightened senses were useless against whatever magic veiled this scent from me.

Evelyn slowed, sniffing the ground, then yipped as she veered sharply to the left. I followed, watching the determination set in her shoulders, the athletic grace with which she navigated the uneven ground. She was a force of nature, unstoppable, yet when we passed the same fallen log twice, frustration crept into her movements as the trail led us in circles.

It doesn't make sense. The scent is here, then it's not, she pushed.

I'm sorry I'm no help. The woods were nearly dark. Evelyn put her nose to the ground and retraced our earlier steps. She turned left like we had the first time, then halted abruptly, her body tensing. She bolted, and I followed. This time, we went north, then curved east. It was when we crossed the creek that recognition tickled the back of my mind.

That scent. I'd missed it the other night when Evelyn and I walked through this same section of woods in our human forms.

Kitimat. Strong and clear.

Evelyn slowed as the trees thinned, and I stopped beside her, following her gaze.

In front of us was Nathan's cabin.

CHAPTER

TWENTY-ONE

I shifted back to my human form, the forest floor cool on my bare feet. I reached back for the backpack. Rowan handed it to me, and I pulled out my clothes, dressing as quickly as possible with my shaking hands.

Why were we here *again?* We'd scouted this place. Every scent was a dead end, and there was nothing to go off of.

But the scent I found was leading straight to it.

We looped the perimeter, this time hearing nothing.

"I unlocked the window again. When we left last time," Rowan whispered.

Last time. I thought of his lips on my skin. His hands curled around my thighs. I had a feeling this was not going to be the same experience.

The pungent odor hit my nose as soon as we stepped inside —that same masked, synthetic scent that had led us here before. I inhaled deeply, trying to pinpoint the source. It seemed to be emanating from the kitchen.

I stomped over, growing more irritated with each step. There was nothing here. I crossed the room and yelped as my foot caught the edge of a rolled corner of the rug. My knees hit the ground with a hollow thud.

I winced, but before I could register the pain in my knees, my wolf whimpered. *I heard it, girl.* I crouched down and flipped up the rug, examining the boards more closely. There. One plank was slightly uneven, the grain not quite matching up with its neighbors. I dug my nails in and pulled.

The board came free with a groan, revealing a dark, gaping hole underneath—a trap door. I growled under my breath. No wonder we hadn't found it last time. It had been concealed so cleverly I never would have noticed if not for the scent.

"Rowan, look at this," I called over my shoulder. "There's a hidden tunnel. The scent is coming from down there."

He came to peer into the darkness beside me. "I don't like this."

"Yeah." I didn't like it either, but what choice did we have? There was something here, I could almost taste it.

Rowan pulled up the next floorboard and lowered himself into the hole. I followed, finding rungs on a solid iron ladder. Rowan's hands were on my waist before I hit the final three steps, and he didn't let go until I was safely on the ground.

The tunnel was narrow and musty, the earthen walls pressing in on either side as we moved deeper underground. The air grew thick and heavy, and the only sound was our muffled footsteps and the occasional drip of water. Even with my enhanced vision, I could barely see a foot in front of me. I kept one hand on the wall, the other outstretched to maintain my balance.

"Remember when we snuck into that abandoned factory as

kids?" Rowan's voice was close. "Looking for buried treasure or something?"

Even though I knew he was trying to distract me, it still worked. I drew a deep breath. "I'm pretty sure the only thing we found was a colony of bats and some rusty nails."

He kept a hand on my lower back as we pressed forward, and after what felt like an eternity, the tunnel began to widen. A faint light appeared ahead.

I held up a hand, signaling Rowan to slow. Cautiously, we inched forward and peeked around the edge into the chamber beyond.

The room was small and bare, lit by a single lamp. The walls were rough-hewn stone, the floor packed dirt. And there, in the center of the chamber, lay a glinting object.

My heart stuttered. It was the dagger. I glanced back at Rowan, seeing my own shock and excitement mirrored in his eyes. Hardly daring to breathe, we stepped into the room. It was empty—nothing to clear.

Rowan gripped my hand as we walked forward, and just as I crouched to pick up the dagger, a strange, sickly sweet scent suddenly flooded the chamber, yanking me out of my trance. I froze, all of my training snapping to the forefront of my mind. *That scent...I knew that scent.*

Six months ago, Bruce and I had responded to an urgent call late one night in Seattle. A routine check for an unresponsive individual.

We'd knocked with no response, then used the landlord's key to enter the small apartment. The air was thick with a sweet, chemical scent that immediately set me on edge, but Bruce was already charging ahead.

I'd called after him, but it was too late. He'd already reached the unconscious man, crouching down to assess him.

A sudden wave of dizziness hit me, and I realized what was

happening. "Fentanyl!" I shouted, but Bruce was already sagging to the floor, the powerful opioid overwhelming him almost instantly.

My heart pounded as I fought to stay conscious. *Who the hell hotboxed an apartment with that shit?* I grabbed my radio, called for backup, and pulled the naloxone from my med kit. I moved quickly, jabbing myself and then pulling Bruce back toward the door to get him out of the contaminated area. The world was spinning, but I administered a dose to him, too.

That had been the second time I'd saved his life.

"Rowan, don't breathe!" I shouted, immediately clamping my mouth shut and holding my breath. My mind raced as I spun around, searching for the source of the vapor. *There wasn't time.*

Panic clawed at my throat as I fumbled for my backpack, my fingers clumsy in my haste. I had to find my medical kit. Had to find the naloxone. It was the only thing that could counteract the fentanyl and buy us enough time to get out of here.

But even as I rummaged through my pack, I could feel the drug beginning to take effect. My head swam, my vision blurring at the edges. *No, no, no.* I gritted my teeth, fighting against the pull of unconsciousness. I had to stay awake. Had to save us.

A thud from behind me. I whirled around to see Rowan crumple to the ground, his eyes rolling back in his head.

"Rowan!" His name tore from my throat in a ragged scream. I lurched toward him, my legs like lead weights. The room tilted and spun around me, the torch flames stretching into dizzying spirals.

I collapsed to my knees beside Rowan, my trembling fingers scrabbling at his neck, desperate to find a pulse. But my own heart was pounding too loudly, drowning out everything else. Black spots danced across my vision, and I felt myself falling, falling...

No. With a burst of determination, I wrenched myself back from the brink. I couldn't pass out. Rowan needed me. We needed each other.

Holding my breath until my lungs burned, I upended my backpack with shaking hands, scattering its contents across the dirt floor. Bandages, antiseptic, painkillers...*there.* My fingers closed around the small naloxone kit.

Put on your own oxygen mask first.

But even as I fumbled to open it, I could feel my grip on consciousness slipping. The edges of my vision tunneled, narrowing to a pinpoint. Rowan's face swam in and out of focus, his features slack and pale.

I had to...had to...

The naloxone slipped from my numb fingers as the darkness rushed up to claim me.

CHAPTER

TWENTY-TWO

Rowan

The world around me started to fracture like a shattered mirror. Vibrant hues of redwood trees bled into unrecognizable smears, and the bland walls of the room around me blended into a disorienting fog that clawed at my senses. A dull roar filled my ears, distorting into a cacophony that threatened to swallow me whole.

Pain lanced through my skull, sharp and persistent as if my wolf was clawing to break free, to run from whatever was causing this upheaval. But even he seemed lost in the chaos, his primal instincts dampened by whatever magic or ailment gripped me.

I staggered, my legs suddenly insubstantial. I reached out for something, anything solid to anchor myself to reality, but my hands grasped only empty air. As hard as I tried to will my alpha strength to the fore, to command my body to obey, my knees buckled, and the ground rushed up to meet me.

In the fragmented haze of my vision, memories flashed—flickers of life in Black Lake Pack, the faces of those who relied on me, their alpha. The pressures of leadership, the weight of expectations, they all dissolved in this maelstrom, leaving behind a hollow feeling where once there had been purpose.

I didn't care.

None of it mattered.

Who was Rowan Steele without his pack? Without his role as protector and provider?

A phantom sensation brushed against my skin—the touch of a mate I had yet to claim—and it stung with a yearning that felt like another piece of the puzzle slipping away. My thoughts chased the fleeting comfort of that imagined touch, spiraling at dizzying speed.

And then heat exploded in my thigh, sharp and brutal. I gasped, the pain a lifeline that hauled me back from the brink of unconsciousness. My mind cleared, sharpening as if drawn from a sheathe, and I clutched at my leg, probing for the cause of the sting.

"Rowan!" The voice cut through the remnants of my stupor, tethering me to the here and now. It was her. Evelyn.

The sight of her ignited a rush of relief through my veins. Her hazel eyes locked with mine. She was above me. Was I on the ground? How had I gotten there?

I opened my mouth to speak, but then a flicker of movement snagged my attention—a shadow detaching itself from the wall behind her.

I tensed, every muscle coiled tight as instinct screamed a warning through my blood. "Behind you," I managed to growl, my voice low and rough with urgency.

Evelyn didn't hesitate, didn't falter, merely shifted her stance. My wolf bristled beneath my skin, eager to leap forward, teeth bared in defense.

A shifter. In a gas mask.

I forced myself up and lunged, wrapping my arms around his waist and tackling him to the ground. I was weak. Clumsy. My wolf clawed at my consciousness, demanding release, but this fight needed precision over brute strength.

He landed a blow against my temple, and I faltered, then twisted, throwing him sideways. I blocked a kick, pivoting to strike back. I scrambled to my feet and let my instinct guide me as I sidestepped a wild punch. My counter was swift—a palm strike to his sternum that sent the man stumbling backward. He was strong, but I was the alpha for a reason.

"Yield!" Alpha energy poured out of me, and I felt him flinch.

The man lunged, a desperate edge to his movements, but I read them like the open pages of a well-thumbed book. I dodged and wove through his attacks, my own blows landing with satisfying thuds against his flesh. A hook to the gut, a jab to the throat—I was a tempest, relentless and unforgiving.

The taste of victory was on my tongue as the man faltered under the barrage. His breaths were ragged, his stance unsteady. I could end him, let the beast within loose, and watch as he crumbled before me.

But we needed answers.

With a final surge of control, I slammed my fist into the side of his knee, bringing him crashing to the ground with a howl of pain. The fight left his eyes, replaced by the dawning realization of defeat.

I hauled him into the tunnel to get the hell out of whatever mist still hung in the air, then reached down and stripped off his mask.

"Justin." Evelyn hissed his name, then snatched up what looked like an aluminum pill bottle from the dirt floor.

He looked up at me then, hate mingled with fear, and I knew I had won. Not just the fight but the upper hand in whatever game he thought he was playing. This might be his territory, but he attacked my mate, and that meant he would pay.

TWENTY-THREE

EVELYN

The weight of Rowan's presence was a living thing in the cramped room, his strength a palpable force that both grounded me and set my nerves on edge. I leaned back against the wall, trying to steady my breath as I watched him, tall and commanding with those piercing blue eyes that seemed to cut right through the dimness. It was easy to see why the Black Lake Pack followed him so loyally, why I found myself drawn to him despite the chaos swirling around us.

He hauled Justin up and slammed him down onto a chair, yanking his hands back and fastening them with a bungee cord he found in the pantry. "You shift, I tear out your throat."

Justin winced as Rowan knocked his injured knee. I doubted it was an accident. My wolf howled in approval.

I glanced down at the dagger on the table—the one thing

we thought could help us. It was a fake. A decoy. My pulse hammered in my ears, betrayal stinging like a fresh wound. How had we not seen it? How had I let my guard down?

"Start talking," Rowan growled. He pulled out a chair and sat in front of him.

Justin gave us both a look of disdain.

"Where are they?" I snapped.

"Who knows?" Justin drawled, shrugging as best he could with his restraints. "Wolves disappear all the time."

"Not like this," Rowan countered, his tone icy. "Three from the lower province, two from the north. It's no coincidence." He flipped the metal canister in his hand. It had been sitting outside the door in the tunnel. I wanted a better look at it when we were done here.

"Maybe those wolves just wanted to be free," Justin suggested, his eyes boring into mine.

I swallowed hard. "Stop playing games."

Justin's eyes glinted, but he said nothing.

"Talk!" Rowan's command echoed off the walls, his power vibrating through me.

"Fine," Justin spat, the veneer of cockiness slipping. "All I know is that the full moon is important. More than usual." His eyes darted to mine, holding a flicker of something unreadable before he looked away.

"Because?" Rowan prompted, his fists clenched, his knuckles white.

"Because it's the August Moon." Justin spat blood on the kitchen floorboards. "And there's power in that, isn't there? You tell me, Evelyn. It's your birthday soon, isn't it?" His words slithered through the room.

My heart stuttered in my chest, and my blood ran cold. My birthday—how had Nathan woven that into his vile plans?

The memory of Nathan's words clung to me like a shadow

as I paced the room, Rowan's gaze heavy on my back. His obsession with the August Moon—a power he believed could unlock ancient magics—suddenly took on a sinister new meaning. *August.* The month of my birth.

The month Callie was born, too.

A chill skated down my spine as the pieces snapped together with a clarity that left me reeling.

"Rowan." I turned to face him. "He knows. Nathan knows I'm here."

Rowan's eyes narrowed, and a low growl rumbled in his chest. Before I could elaborate, a fist pounded on the front door. Rowan whirled, throwing himself between me and the door.

"Justin! I swear, if you don't open this damn door, I'll—"

Rowan was there, throwing the door wide. I'd recognized Blake's voice, and so had Rowan.

Blake stood in the doorway, heaving like he'd just sprinted through the woods. "What are you doing here?"

Rowan moved, giving Blake a better view of the scene in the kitchen. Blake rushed in, holding out his arms to hug me when Rowan snapped, "Don't touch her, Ash."

Blake froze. "I'm just glad she's okay."

"Be glad on the other side of the counter."

Blake's nostrils flared, but he nodded once and did as he said.

I swallowed hard. "Blake, I think—"

"Nathan has Callista," he finished, throwing his arm out and clamping his hand around Justin's throat. "If anything happens to her, I'll kill you both."

Rowan didn't stop him. Even when Justin's face turned purple and he made a sound that made my insides twist. Finally, Blake dropped his hand. "Where is he."

Justin's eyes were bloodshot. He coughed, trying to drag air into his lungs.

Blake barely let him recover before slamming his fist into Justin's stomach. "I asked you a question!"

"Blake, stop." I took a step toward him. "For all we know, Nathan's forced his pack to comply with whatever this is." I didn't know if I believed Justin was only obeying orders, but I'd had enough experience with Nathan's manipulation to give him the benefit of the doubt.

Plus, we didn't need him. I knew where Nathan would be.

"He'll be at Whiteswan," I said. The place that Nathan would seek out was a geothermal pool nestled in the Rockies. It was known for its healing properties. Nathan had talked about it obsessively, how the magic pulsed through the earth, alive and breathing, how the veil grew thin there.

I thought he'd been speaking in hypotheticals.

Until he'd tried to haul me there against my will. Until he'd tried to force me to bond with him under the full moon.

That was the last night I'd spent with Kitimat Pack.

"Lyra spoke of blood and sacrifice," I whispered, recalling the witch's words. "It has to be there, Rowan."

CHAPTER
TWENTY-FOUR

I hated every second I had to be away from her. Especially knowing that someone had been in my damn house. I needed to seal our bond, but more than that, my wolf wanted blood. I would let him have it as soon as we figured out who the hell was behind this mess. I had my guesses, but couldn't decide if I wanted to be right.

Nathan Black would pay for what he did to Evelyn and for his involvement with the dagger. But was he following orders? Was he so blinded by power he'd gotten wrapped up in dark magic himself? Would he put his entire pack at risk for his own gain? The idea made my stomach twist.

Lana nudged my shoulder. "You good?"

"What do you think?"

She nodded, and I leaned over the sturdy oak table, arms crossed, eyes scanning my most trusted allies. I hated that after the dagger had gone missing, I questioned whether that trust was misplaced.

Evelyn didn't recognize the scent, I reminded myself. Even though it was masked, she would've known if it were someone in my pack, wouldn't she? I had to make a choice, and for better or worse, I was choosing them.

"Whiteswan Lake." I watched their expressions as they took in the words.

Tori's lips pursed. "That place is sacred."

"You think he's taking the dagger *there?*" Mara talked over her.

"Evelyn's sure." I shuddered as my wolf gnashed his teeth. As our bond strengthened, I felt more from her, and the sensations that flooded the bond as she spoke of the pools made my spine turn to ice. Nathan had planned to take *her* there. To force her into being his mate.

"Ready to crash their party?" Lana quipped, but her humor didn't quite reach her eyes.

"Something like that." My jaw tightened at the thought of Evelyn caught in the middle of this mess. I met each gaze in turn, letting them see my resolve. "They're going to be ready for us."

Nathan knows I'm here. I needed to hit something.

"Easy." Jasper braved a hand on my shoulder, and I flinched. "You'll get your moment, Alpha. I swear it."

"Anyone want to fill me in on the actual plan?" Lana muttered.

"Simple," I growled. "We take the fight to them before they can bring it to us."

"Suicide mission, then?" Jasper's eyes gleamed. "Just another Friday."

"Better than waiting for whatever power they're working to unleash," I shot back. He was kidding, but I wasn't in the mood. Especially since Blake Ash was insisting on being a part of our group. "We've got forty-eight hours." That damn clock ticked in the back of my mind. *Two days.* I only had two more than that. If Evelyn didn't accept our mating bond—if we didn't consummate it—it would begin to fade for her. I couldn't accept that, but I also wouldn't force her paw. My wolf whimpered at the thought.

Mara's face hardened. "I'm ready to tear Nathan apart."

"You can start with Justin." Tori's eyes flashed. "We have him sedated and restrained. Happy to let you have a go."

Blake had already called dibs on him, and I was happy to acquiesce. I wondered how much it was costing him to betray his alpha. As third of Kitimat, he had to be suffering. I didn't fully trust him like Evelyn did, but I could respect him for that. Just like I respected Evelyn for finding a way out.

"Patience." I lowered my voice. "We move as one, or not at all."

The meeting broke soon after. I was the last to leave, the weight of leadership heavy on my shoulders. As I passed through the doorway, Jasper's voice halted my exit.

"Rowan." He jogged up behind me. "What's your play?"

"I already told you—"

"No, dipshit. Your play with Evelyn. If I keep feeling all of this—" He circled his hand over my chest, "through our bond? I'm going to lose my everloving mind. Or sleep with someone I shouldn't."

"Please don't piss off the mayor again."

Jasper threw his hands out. "I'm just sayin'. Under your control, buddy."

I scoffed. "Clearly."

"You need to lay all that alpha charm on thick."

Terrible advice. That was probably the worst thing I could do with Evelyn, but I didn't correct him. Jasper hadn't found his mate yet, either, and he only wanted to help. "Thanks, bud."

"Worst case, she dumps your ass, right?" He gave a lopsided smile that I guessed was supposed to be comforting.

"You say that like it won't damn me to an eternity of loneliness."

Jasper clapped his hands on my shoulders. "You'll never be lonely. And there are plenty of she-wolves that would be happy to—"

"Not going to happen." I clenched my fists at my sides. I knew what he was thinking. Our pack was already struggling. We needed new strength. New numbers. As alpha, I would need to strengthen the pack. I'd need to procreate.

Revulsion twisted in my gut. "The thought of taking anyone else..." I couldn't finish. It was unthinkable. The very idea scraped against my insides like thorns. My wolf snarled within, possessive and single-minded. "I'll win her over," I vowed, more to myself than to Jasper. Something flickered in his eyes. "What?"

He took a step back, shoving his hands in his pocket. "I'd never question you. Never. But as your second, I have to ask you to consider—"

"Spit it out, Jasper."

"Can she commit to this pack? She sure as hell seems strong enough to lead if she can keep you at arm's length, but will she be loyal?"

I ground my teeth at the criticism, but it was a fair question. One I had to consider. "I'll make sure. Before we bond."

"Even if she's topless?"

I shoved Jasper against the closest tree.

THE PUB's dim light spilled onto the street as Jasper and I approached. I pushed the door open, and the scent of beer, peanut shells, and warm bodies hit me like a physical force, carrying with it the undercurrents of *her*.

My eyes dragged to her like iron filing under a magnet. Her long, auburn hair cascaded down her back as she leaned over the pool table, cue in hand. Eyes focused, mouth slightly parted, her ass tilted in a way that made my jeans tighten.

Her shot was smooth, precise, but her shoulders never relaxed as she stood. I loved that she was there with my pack. Loved that she still trusted them even after the events of that night. The fact that she wasn't at home curled up after the attack at the cabin showed her strength. It showed her desire for a pack, even if she didn't know it yet.

"She's trying to unwind," Jasper murmured beside me.

"Trying and failing."

She straightened up, revealing the faint crease between her brows, the subtle clench of her jaw. Will laughed at something she said, and though she smiled back, it didn't reach her eyes.

The pull of her hit every fiber of my being, an invisible tether that yanked at my chest with every breath she took. It was painful to watch her like this, wrapped in layers of stress she couldn't shake off. My wolf prowled restlessly within, instincts screaming to go to her, comfort her, protect her.

"You've got a little—" Jasper reached up, pretending to wipe drool from my mouth.

I slapped his hand away. "Asshole."

His chuckle faded behind me as I stepped forward, closing the distance between us. Evelyn straightened up and turned, her hazel eyes locking onto mine. There was a flash of something—surprise, maybe even a hint of pleasure—before she schooled her expression into one of casual indifference.

"Mind if I watch?" I leaned against the edge of the pool table.

"Only if you promise not to critique my technique," she shot back.

"Wouldn't dream of it," I grinned, watching as she chalked the tip of her cue stick. "Although, if you wanted a few pointers, I'm sure I could—"

"From you?" Evelyn raised an eyebrow, amusement flickering in her eyes. "The last time you played me in pool, I recall a certain someone ripping the felt."

"That was one time. The table was defective."

Will laughed next to her. "I want to hear this story."

Evelyn shot me a look. "I'm sure Rowan can tell you his version."

"What, not in the mood to embarrass me?"

Her lips twitched as she drew a deep breath. "Not in the mood for much of anything, to be honest."

I ached to wrap her in my arms. She was putting on a strong face, but I sensed the grief and fear hovering just below the surface.

I took a step closer. "Right now we're safe—"

"I swear, Rowan, if you tell me to 'live laugh love' or be present, I'm going to stab you with this poolstick."

I knew what she was doing. What she'd always done. She was collecting evidence for why this life—this place—was worth running from. But I wasn't going to let her slip through my fingers.

I glanced around at the small group of my wolves, their eyes trained on me. Waiting for my response. I walked behind Evelyn and picked up a pool cue. "I spent a long time waiting for things to settle after the packs split. If Kitimat stopped trying to spread their lies, then I could breathe. When my pack saw me as their rightful alpha, I could sleep at night. The truth is, we're shifters. Our world is never going to be settled. There will always be another threat. But it doesn't mean we can't enjoy every damn moment in between."

Evelyn's eyes were fixed on me as I chalked the end of my cue.

"Want to play?" I asked. I was running out of time. I could feel her pulling back. Explaining away the moments we had in the cabin, the connection she felt at the picnic. I didn't blame her, but I had to change the story in her head.

Not all packs were toxic.

Not all alphas would take advantage of her or anyone else.

She looked at me through her lashes. "What do you think a game of pool is going to contribute to this situation?"

I leaned in, my lips brushing the shell of her ear. "Not just pool, Strawberry. I'm challenging you to a game of *strip* pool."

Her eyebrows arched. When she spoke, she kept her voice low. "After what just happened, you want to play strip pool? Here?" She motioned to my pack and the rest of the pub, full to the brim with folks from town.

"Scared you'll lose?"

My wolves hooted and hollered around us. It wasn't often that the Evelyn Berry I knew backed down from a challenge, and I was counting on that streak of defiance to work in my favor.

Her lips pressed into a thin line, the barest hint of a smile tugging at the corners. I could see the war behind her eyes, the desire to throw caution to the wind.

"Scared I'll embarrass you in front of your loyal followers, more like," she muttered, though her gaze lingered on the pool table, weighing the offer. "But fine. Have it your way."

Will pulled up a stool for Marissa, and Liam grabbed a few extra for him and his friends.

"Call the ball, call the pocket," I said, moving behind her

and pretending I didn't have much space so I had an excuse to drag my hand over her hip and press up against her tight jeans. There was that damn flush on her skin that was going to undo me.

"Don't think I'll make this easy for you." She grabbed the triangle rack and started dropping in balls.

"Wouldn't dream of it."

CHAPTER
TWENTY-FIVE

The cue ball cracked against the striped orange ball, sending it careening toward the far corner pocket. I held my breath, willing it to drop. At the last second, it caught the edge and bounced out. *Damn.*

Rowan's low chuckle sent a shiver down my spine. "Tough luck there, Strawberry." His blue eyes sparkled with mischief.

I winked at him. "Don't get too comfy."

Rowan shook his head as he circled the pool table, sizing up his shot. The dim lighting of the pub cast shadows across his chiseled features. Something in the way he carried himself made my insides liquify. It couldn't be summed up as mere confidence. It was more than that. It was raw power barely contained. Like a shaken up Coke. I wondered what would happen if I popped that tab.

I tossed my hair over my shoulder, hoping nobody would notice my blush. "Are you wearing any jewelry, Rowan?"

He grunted. "Don't distract me."

"Oh, I'm not trying to distract you." I leaned low over the side of the pool table, knowing exactly how much of my bra would be peeking out of my shirt right about then.

Rowan's eyes flicked up. His hand tightened on his pool cue. Without breaking eye contact, he said, "Seven. Side pocket." He took the shot and sank the ball. My mouth went dry.

My stomach swooped, and adrenaline pumped through my veins, making me heady. The air between us practically crackled. As a lone wolf, I was used to keeping others at a distance, but Rowan drew me in like a moth to a flame.

I knew it was mostly the bond to blame. Mostly. I also knew if I held out long enough, that would start to fade. I'd intended to do just that. Stay away from him. Focus on finding Callista. Get back to Seattle. But now...

Rowan straightened up and flashed me a devastating grin, his eyes burning into mine.

I exhaled and reached up to my right ear.

His smile faltered. "Earrings don't count."

"They sure as hell do count," Mia called out.

Rowan shot her a look. "Whose side are you on?"

Mia pointed at me, and I laughed, setting my earring on the closest table. "Keep that safe for me."

"Both." Rowan tapped his cue on the floor.

I frowned. "What do you—"

"If earrings count, it has to be both."

I reached up and took off my second earring. "Fine."

Rowan nodded, satisfied, then took his next shot. It was ambitious, and he missed.

I swallowed hard and picked up my cue, determined to wipe that sexy smirk off his face. *Game on.* I stepped up to the pool table, my focus narrowing to the colored balls scattered across the green felt. The cue stick felt solid and smooth beneath my fingers.

I leaned down, took aim, called my shot, and struck the cue ball. It connected with a sharp crack, sending the three-ball rolling toward the corner pocket. For a breathless moment, I thought it wouldn't drop, but at the last second, it toppled over the edge.

Whoops and cheers erupted from the pack members clustered around the pool table as I bent to line up my next shot. Their raucous encouragement only stoked the flames. I wanted to beat him.

"Take it off, Rowan!" Jace hollered, his grin wolfish.

Heat flooded my cheeks. Don't get me wrong, I wanted to see him. *All* of him. Which caught me off guard. After Nathan, the idea of being intimate with anyone shut me down like pressing a power button on a computer. But after Rowan had spent time discovering nearly every inch of me in the cabin, my screen was suddenly back on.

I felt safe with him.

That in and of itself was a miracle. He'd had every opportunity to force me to submit to him, and he'd never taken advantage. He had a damn mating bond in his pocket—a justifiable reason to push me—and still, he'd allowed me to be the one in control.

Ironically, that only made me want to move over and let him sit in the driver's seat.

As Rowan reached over his back and pulled his shirt over his head in one smooth motion, my breath caught in my throat. Sweet moon above. I'd imagined Rowan shirtless countless times over the past few days, but the reality put every fantasy to shame. Golden skin stretched taut over chiseled muscle, his abs so defined they deserved their own zip code. And those tattooed sleeves hugging his bulging biceps...I wanted to trace every swirl and whorl with my tongue.

And the way he undressed? That was stupid hot. I suddenly didn't want to be in this packed pub.

I wanted him to do that again.

Just for me.

Rowan looked up, and by his devilish grin, he knew exactly what effect he was having on me. My wolf was *panting,* and he could feel it.

I kept my eyes fixed firmly on the cue ball, trying to ignore the heat between my thighs. Hard to do when I had to walk up to the table.

Rowan chuckled, low and dark, as he braced his hands on the polished wood. "Two can play at this game."

"I don't know what you're talking about." I forced my eyes to stay put and then sucked in a breath as a wave of heat pulsed through me, flooding from my head to my toes. *Holy shit.* My eyes snapped up. "What the hell?" I hissed.

Rowan smiled innocently. "I don't know what you're talking about."

I swallowed hard, trying to clear my blurring vision. Never in my life had I been *this* turned on before. I could feel him—sense his longing through our solidifying bond—and I was not equipped to handle it. Images of him throwing me onto the pool table and claiming me right there in front of everyone flashed in my head, and I couldn't make them leave. Didn't *want* to make them leave. I was going to combust. That or throw my cue down on the floor and jump him like a wolf in heat.

I jolted as something ice cold hit my neck. My eyes closed involuntarily as Rowan's hand ran an ice cube up and down the ridges of my spine, slipping his fingers beneath the fabric of my tank top. "It's a bit hot in here, don't you think?"

"Mmm." I could barely make my voice work. My breath came in quick bursts as the melting ice dripped down my back.

Rowan pulled it from my skin, then waited until I looked up to place the half-melted ice cube on his tongue. He stood there in front of me and sucked on it. "It's still your shot."

Dead. I was dead.

"Don't you dare let him win, Evelyn!" a young wolf standing next to Mia called out.

I looked up to see we'd attracted not only the rest of the pack but plenty of mundanes as well. They clinked their glasses and egged me on. I turned back to Rowan. He was shirtless, and I was only missing my earrings.

I stood straight, reached into the glass of whatever the hell he was drinking and stole an ice cube, popping it in my mouth. I leaned in close and whispered, "Thanks for the reminder," then flicked my ice cold tongue against his neck.

Rowan reached for my waist, but I slipped out of his grip and lined up my next shot. I gritted my teeth, calling into play every crisis skill I'd ever utilized on an emergency call. With a sharp crack, I sent the cue ball careening into the six-ball. It dropped neatly into the corner pocket.

I straightened and shot Rowan a triumphant look. "I believe you owe me an article of clothing, alpha."

His eyes never left mine as he flicked the button open on his jeans. The women started catcalling, and my wolf growled. *Mine.* I shook myself. *Not mine,* I shot back. Not yet, at least. I was still planning to go back to Seattle. No matter how much I wanted Rowan Steele, I couldn't stay here. Not with Nathan less than twenty minutes away, and not when being with him could mean an all-out pack war. I wouldn't do that to him or his wolves.

But then his jeans were puddled on the ground, and that time, I couldn't keep my eyes on the pool balls. I scanned his body, taking in his tight, black boxer briefs and eeeeverything they were barely containing.

"Like what you see?" Rowan asked with a self-assured smirk that made me want to smack him. Or jump his bones. You know, options.

"One more shot, Evelyn!" Jasper hooted.

He was right. One more, and I would win...and Rowan would have to drop his boxers. I started to sweat. I lined up the shot, but my hands were shaking so hard I could barely hold the stick steady. I drew a deep breath and struck, but the cue ball missed my intended target.

Rowan brushed against me as he strutted over to set his glass down and pick up his cue. "My turn."

He didn't waste a breath before knocking the ten-ball into the far pocket. He stood, his eyes darkening as he nodded to my shirt. "No more jewelry?"

No more jewelry, damn it. I crossed my arms and tugged my tank top over my head. Cool air kissed my overheated skin as I tossed it aside, leaving me in just my black lace bra. Rowan had already seen my body, but it felt different here.

His eyes darkened to cobalt as his gaze drifted down my body, all the men in the pub cheering him on.

"He won't make the next one!" Mia jeered.

But Rowan wasn't messing around now. He lowered himself over the table. "Twelve. Back right." Crack. He sent it off the side wall, spinning right where he'd called it.

Heat bloomed beneath my skin as Rowan stalked toward me, his movements fluid and predatory. I stood my ground, refusing to back down even as my heart hammered against my ribcage. He stopped mere inches away, close enough that I could feel the warmth radiating off his bare chest. "Pants."

I undid the button on my jeans and pulled them over my hips, but Rowan stopped my hands. "I'll take it from here." He dragged the fabric down my thighs, over my knees and calves, then waited for me to step out. Once I did, he threw my jeans next to his.

My heart pounded in my chest. I stood in my lace boy shorts in front of an entire pub, and Rowan wasn't missing. "Rowan—"

He stalked away from me and called another shot, then lined up his stick and—

Missed.

My pulse fluttered in my throat. Rowan straightened, locking his eyes on mine. "Looks like it's your shot."

Had he done that on purpose? He'd just proven that he could make whatever shot he wanted, and then...

"Take him, Evelyn!"

"You only need one shot to win this!"

I didn't know who was yelling through the din, but I grabbed my stick and assessed the table. When I saw where the cue ball ended up, my eyes found Rowan's.

Did you set this up? I didn't realize I'd pushed my voice into his head until his eyes widened and his lips parted. How had I done that? When I'd tried before, it felt like I was hitting a brick wall, but now it felt like blowing water through a straw.

Why would I do that? I'm only in my boxers, Rowan sent back.

I glanced back at the table. He'd done this on purpose. I was sure of it. There was no better place for that cue ball for my next shot.

But why?

"Take the shot!"

"Bury him!"

Blood rushed in my ears as I bent over and called the shot, then struck. The ball sank, and before I could stand up, Rowan's hands slid around my waist, his touch scorching. Wolf whistles and cheers erupted around us.

"Why did you do that?" I whispered.

Rowan's voice was low. "You'll never have to wonder if I'll take the fall for you." He stepped back and dropped his boxers. The cheers were deafening, and my brain short-circuited. Rowan Steele, naked as the day he was born, in front of his entire pack. In front of the entire pub.

For me.

It was the ultimate display of vulnerability from an alpha. Of trust. My tough shell of a heart cracked wide open, every protective instinct surging to the surface. I wanted to cherish him, worship him, claim him as mine.

Right this second.

When our gazes locked again, the rest of the world fell away. Nothing existed except the two of us and the electric current flowing between us. I took a shuddering breath, struggling for control. "Can you give me a ride home?"

Rowan's mouth quirked. "Do you want—"

"Now. Please."

His grin widened. He quickly pulled up his boxers and grabbed the rest of our clothes, then grabbed my hand and pulled me to the door.

CHAPTER

TWENTY-SIX

My heart pounded against my ribs as we ran out the door, hoots and hollers following us out into the night.

"Hell of a game, Rowan!" Liam called after me, grinning.

"You're welcome!" I threw them a sly smile over my shoulder as I guided Evelyn to my truck with a possessive hand at the small of her back. She was still in her underwear, and I was more than okay with that. Opening the passenger door, I helped her inside with a hand cupping her upper thigh.

The instant I slid behind the wheel and started the engine, Evelyn transformed before my eyes. Gone was the cautious, reserved she-wolf. A wild, feral creature sat in her place, eyes blazing with untamed desire.

Her hand crept up my thigh, sending sparks through my

164

body. I sucked in a sharp breath as I backed up and pulled out of the parking lot. "Evelyn—"

But she was already crawling into my lap, straddling me, pinning me back against the seat. Her mouth claiming mine in a searing kiss that obliterated every thought.

Blindly, I yanked the wheel to the side, bringing the truck to a screeching halt on the shoulder a block from the pub. I was panting as I wrenched my lips from hers.

"I won't take you for the first time in my damn truck."

She attacked my mouth again, hands fisting in my hair. "I don't care where," she growled against my lips. "I just need you. Now."

With a groan, I surrendered to the inferno raging between us. Our tongues battled for dominance as I gripped her hips, grinding her against me.

This was madness. The lust. The need. I'd never experienced anything like it. Every fiber of my being screamed to make her mine.

But I can't. Not yet.

My wolf howled inside me, a primal need to claim our mate thundering through my veins. But a tiny, rational part of me resisted. I gentled my touch, stroking her back as I slowed our frenzied kisses.

"Evelyn, look at me," I rasped.

When her eyes opened, the blend of green and gold was nearly swallowed by black. The same desire, need, and desperation. I saw it all reflected there and felt it radiating through our bond.

I pushed a stray tendril of hair from her face. "I want you more than my next breath. But not like this. Not something quick and rough. When we bond, I'm going to take my time. I'm going to worship every inch of you."

She shivered, her voice husky. "Then take me home, Rowan."

I nearly came undone right there on the side of the road. The urge to give in, to lose myself in her, was overwhelming. But her safety came first. Always.

"I need to know this is truly what you want." My voice was hoarse. "That you're ready to belong to me, body and soul. Because once I claim you, there's no going back. Not for me."

Uncertainty flickered in her eyes and she bit her lip. She tried to mask it, but didn't recover fast enough. "If you're asking if I want you…" She dropped her head, running her tongue over my lower lip.

She knew what I was asking, and that wasn't the answer I longed to hear, but it was enough for this moment. I couldn't push her. I wouldn't risk scaring her off. I wrapped my arms around her waist and squeezed, then helped her back to her seat and waited for her to buckle up.

I could barely see straight as I put the truck into gear and peeled away from the shoulder, tires spitting gravel. The drive back to my place was a blur, my focus split between the road and the maddening temptation beside me. Evelyn's hand rested high on my thigh, tracing idle patterns that sent jolts of electricity straight to my core.

Keep it together. I reprimanded myself even as a low growl built in my throat. My wolf paced restlessly beneath my skin, desperate to lay claim to our mate. *Soon*, I promised him. And I believed it. Every day Evelyn drew closer. Every day, she let a little more of her guard down.

What felt like an eternity later, we pulled up to my door. I barely had the engine off before Evelyn was out of her seat belt straddling my lap, her lips finding mine again in a searing kiss. I groaned into her mouth, my hands spanning her waist, the heat of her sinking into my palms.

"Inside," I rumbled between kisses, grasping for some semblance of control. She reluctantly slid off my lap, and we stumbled out of the truck. I reached back in to snag our clothes off the seat and followed her up the steps with unsteady legs.

The moment we crossed through the door, I dropped everything and pressed her back against it, caging her in with my arms. I drew a deep, shuddering breath, struggling to master myself. I wanted her so badly I was shaking with it. But I couldn't consummate our bond fully. Not until I knew she was ready. Not until I knew she was fully mine.

Evelyn trusted me. She wanted me. But something was holding her back, and I knew exactly what it was.

Nathan Black.

Kitimat Pack.

She'd left to escape them, and they still loomed over us like a shadow. So tonight, I would show her what she had to look forward to. Then tomorrow, I'd do whatever it took to make her safe here in Black Lake.

"I'm going to take such good care of you, Evelyn." I nuzzled into her throat, reveling in the sigh that left her lips. Picking her up, I carried her to the bedroom and laid her back on the bed. My bed. *Where she belongs.* The possessive thought sent a thrill through me.

I took my time undressing her, revealing her curves inch by tantalizing inch until she was bared before me, flushed and wanting. My eyes drank their fill, committing every detail to memory.

"So beautiful," I breathed.

I worshipped her slowly with hands and mouth, stoking the flames higher and higher. Each breathy sigh and moan I coaxed from her lips sweeter than the last. I picked up where I'd left off in the cabin and learned her body like a map—every freckle, every sensitive spot. The sounds she made when I touched her just right.

Her taste on my tongue was pure ambrosia, and I toyed with her until she was writhing. Until the only word falling from her lips was my name, a desperate prayer. Every beat of her heart thudded through me, and as she released control, her ache and desire flooded our bond like I'd broken through a dam.

I flowed with that current, responding to every want, every ache, until she arched off the bed, shattering apart in my arms. I pulled her into my chest as she shuddered and rode out the waves. "I've got you. I've always got you."

As she lay there quivering and boneless, I quickly shucked off my own clothes and wrapped her body with my own. She tipped her chin, and our eyes locked, the rest of the world falling away.

In that moment, nothing existed but her. Us.

I pulled her close, and we rested tangled together, gasping for breath. I felt her heartbeat gradually slowing beneath my cheek where it rested on her chest.

"Rowan," she whispered, threading her fingers through my hair. "That was..."

"Yeah." I lifted my head to meet her gaze, stunned anew by the vulnerability I saw there. The trust. I brushed a thumb over her kiss-swollen lower lip.

She reached up to cup my face in her hands. "Can I please—"

I shook my head. *No.* My wolf growled, pressing forward until I could barely keep him at bay. *NO.* I couldn't solidify this bond until she was sure. If she left now, I would be torn apart. But if she left after that? I didn't know if I could survive it.

Her eyes were glassy. "I want you. All of you. But..." She bit her lip, hesitating.

I kissed her forehead. "I know." A piece clicked into place in my heart. She wanted *me*. She would choose me. But I had to make her and my pack safe first.

I was the alpha. That responsibility had never rested so heavy on my shoulders.

As she drifted off to sleep in my arms, a sense of rightness, of completion, settled into my bones. I didn't have all the answers, but this was exactly where I was meant to be. Where we were meant to be.

Together.

As the first rays of dawn filtered through the curtains, I extracted myself from Evelyn's warm embrace. She murmured but didn't wake, her face peaceful and content. I could watch her like that for hours, but there was work to be done.

Silently, I moved about the house, gathering supplies. My mind raced with plans and contingencies, mapping out every possible scenario. We were heading into the unknown, and I'd be damned if I let anything happen to Evelyn or our pack.

There was a soft knock at the door at ten, and I jogged as soundlessly as possible over my hardwood floors, opening it for Finn. I stepped out on the porch.

"What do you think?" I glanced down at the metal canister in his hands.

"I've never seen anything like it." Finn handed me the jar Lyra had given me, the liquid now at a lower level. "Rowan, you have to be careful. I haven't had enough time to test this."

I nodded, taking the canister from him. "It works?"

"Yeah. It's aerosolized. But—"

"Got it." I pulled him into a quick hug. It wasn't that I was hiding this work from Evelyn or my pack, but Lyra had given the jar to me. I'd felt something when our fingers had brushed, not strong enough to be a message, more like an impression. This was for me and me alone.

As soon as Finn left, my thoughts drifted to the night before, to the feel of Evelyn's skin against mine, the taste of her on my tongue. I shook my head, trying to focus.

But even as I strategized and planned, part of me was still back in that bed, holding the woman I loved. The woman I'd die to protect. My mate, in every sense of the word.

I finished my preparations and made us breakfast just as Evelyn began to stir. I felt her awareness surfacing in the other room.

Grabbing the plate with eggs and sausage, I strode back to my bedroom and perched on the edge of the bed, brushing a strand of hair from her face. "Morning, beautiful."

She blinked up at me, a slow smile spreading across her lips. "Morning." Then she took in my appearance, the packed bags against the wall outside the bedroom door, and her expression sobered. "Is it time?"

I nodded solemnly. "It's time. We have to move." I took her hand, lacing our fingers. "But I want breakfast with you first."

CHAPTER

TWENTY-SEVEN

Every crackle of a branch underfoot felt like the ticking of a clock counting down to the confrontation we were approaching. Evelyn's hand sought mine, her grip tight and grounding. Our footsteps were silent, barely whispering against the blanket of fallen leaves as we advanced toward the geothermal pools through the woods.

Nathan knows I'm here. Evelyn's words circled back to me. We had Justin, which meant Nathan had to know our plans. From the sounds of it, he'd welcomed them.

That sent ice slipping down my spine. There was so much we hadn't understood, and we still didn't have satisfactory answers. I worried we were walking straight into a trap.

I hadn't wanted Evelyn to come, but she refused to be left behind. Truthfully, I'd had no argument when she'd argued that Nathan might've wanted to separate us. I didn't have any answers, and that was eating me alive. The only thought I clung to was trusting my mate. If I was going to ask her to lead Black Lake with me, then that trust had to start now.

Above us, the moon rose, a massive orb casting an ethereal glow through the trees. Its light seemed to hum with power, coating everything in a silver sheen that made our already heightened senses sing. Energy coursed through me, a torrent of strength and raw dominance that surged to new heights knowing my mate was next to me. Possibly at risk.

Positions, I pushed to my pack, a chorus of affirmatives echoing back to me in a symphony of mental whispers. We moved separately but as one, shadows flitting between the redwoods. Each member knew their role. Tori and Mara rounded north. Jasper moved west and Lana east with their handful of wolves. I was with Evelyn on the south side. Everyone was on the lookout for scouts and Nathan's enforcers.

Blake had given us all the information he could, which meant we should get through their patrols without an altercation. All of it made me nervous. He'd offered to stay back with Justin, but that sent off warning bells in my head. Kitimat guarding Kitimat? After he'd given us intel? Hell, no. No matter how much Evelyn trusted him, and no matter how much motivation he had to betray his alpha, I wasn't leaving that much up to chance.

Liam, Finn, and two other enforcers from Black Lake were guarding Tori's. Jasper had the pleasure of babysitting Blake. If anything went wrong, I trusted my second.

Evelyn stayed close, her presence a constant flame at my side. The connection between us pulsed with every heartbeat, a tangible thing that had only deepened after last night. The memory of her next to me, the taste of her skin, the sound of her pleasure—it all lingered, fueling my need to shield her from whatever darkness we were about to face.

East flank ready, Lana's voice cut through the mental link, her position secure.

West in position, Jasper added.

North secure, Tori reported, her message only flowing through me. She wasn't linked to the rest of my pack, and if I was ever released as her regional second, I'd no longer have access to her communication. I was grateful for it now.

South is clear, I responded, my voice a low growl even in the mindscape. My eyes flickered to Evelyn, her gaze meeting mine. My own determination was mirrored there, along with a fierce courage that made pride swell within my chest.

We strike as one, I reminded them all, my alpha command reverberating through the pack bond.

The forest held its breath, the air thick with the scent of mulch and pine as we approached the edge of the trees.

"Rowan," Evelyn whispered beside me, her voice barely audible above the rustle of leaves. Her hand brushed against mine, a fleeting touch that sent a jolt of electricity up my arm. I nodded, tightening my grip on the mental reins of my wolf. He strained beneath the surface, eager to leap forth and claim his territory. But not yet. Control was crucial, and I'd been getting a hell of a lot of practice.

We edged forward, our steps careful and quiet despite the urgency pumping through our veins. Then we saw him—Nathan Black, his rugged form outlined by the ghostly light, his black hair and dark eyes almost blending into the dark tapestry of the night.

He smells like shit, Jasper sent through the bond. I almost snorted.

Body at his feet, Tori's thought flashed through the link, sharp and quick.

My gaze dropped, and there it was—a body slumped on the ground, ominously still. Rage and disgust flared within me, hot and demanding. This was not the way of the pack. We were guardians, protectors. *What had led Nathan to this?*

Evelyn's hand flew to her mouth.

Steady, I commanded through the link, my alpha authority wrapping around each pack member. *Wait for my signal.*

Every muscle coiled, ready to strike, but we needed answers first. Nathan was an arrogant asshole, but an outright executioner? I didn't cast it out of the realm of possibility, but I didn't want to believe it. I didn't want to believe any shifter, especially an alpha, could turn on his own.

Is he alive? Evelyn's question was a whisper in my mind.

I moved closer, shifting to get a better view.

Then Nathan turned. The dagger in his right hand, though it looked different now. Dark on the blade.

And that's when I saw her. Long, dark curls splayed out around the figure on the ground. A slash of red blooming at her throat.

The flashes from Evelyn that had filtered through our bond replayed in my mind. Nathan standing over her. Nathan's hand bruising her arm. Nathan pushing her up against the wall and—

The last threads of my control snapped, and though I'd given the order to wait just moments before, all I saw was red.

CHAPTER
TWENTY-EIGHT

Rowan charged forward, abandoning all pretense of following the plan. Without thinking, I raced after him, my heart in my throat. Nathan pivoted to face us, not a hint of surprise on his cruel features. As if he'd been expecting us all along.

I stumbled as a wave of alpha energy crashed over me like a tsunami. I'd felt alphas before. Nathan had used his power to command, and while Rowan had never forced me into compliance, I sensed his energy the moment I passed him at that Tim Hortons. It was like standing out in the cool night air and then moving under a heat lamp.

This was nothing like that. My knees buckled at the weight of it. Nathan's dominance was overwhelming, oppressive, threatening to crush me under its weight.

"What the hell?" I gasped.

Rowan staggered slightly before regaining his footing. His eyes widened when he saw me, and he sidestepped to stand between me and Nathan. He shook his head, jaw clenched. My gaze fell on the body sprawled before Nathan's feet. *No*, I silently pleaded. *Please don't let it be her.*

I squinted, trying to make out any identifying features in the dim moonlight filtering through the trees. Desperate to prove it wasn't Callie lying there broken and lifeless.

My wolf knew before I did. The smell was off. Hair color, too. Then I spotted her—Callista. Bound to a tree several yards away, her head lolling to the side. Relief flooded me, followed swiftly by fresh panic.

"Callie!" I lunged forward, but Rowan's arm shot out, holding me back.

Nathan's cruel chuckle sliced through the tense silence. "Well, well. The prodigal daughter returns." His hazel eyes glinted with malice as they fixed on me. "Did you miss me, Evelyn?"

I could barely hear him over the frantic pounding of my own heart. The sickening dread knotting in my stomach. All I knew was that I had to get to her. I had to save my friend from this monster wearing a man's skin.

Rowan stepped fully in front of me, eclipsing me from Nathan's predatory gaze. "Leave her out of this."

"Oh, but she's already so deeply involved, isn't she?" Nathan crooned. He began to circle us slowly, each deliberate step sending my pulse racing. "In fact, I'd say she's the guest of honor at tonight's little celebration."

"What the hell are you talking about?" Rowan snarled.

Nathan's thin lips curled into a spine-chilling smile. "While you two were busy playing house, I've been rather productive." He nudged the prone figure with his boot.

My blood turned to ice in my veins.

"You're a sick bastard if you call that an accomplishment," Rowan bit out, every word trembling with barely leashed fury.

Nathan's eyes flicked between the two of us, and his expression darkened. "One more accomplishment than you've had, it seems." His eyes bore into me. "But she-wolves always love alphas to prove their strength, right Evelyn?"

Rowan's fists clenched so tight his knuckles turned white. I grabbed onto his arm to steady myself. No. *No, no, no.* This couldn't be happening. The world seemed to tilt and spin around me. I thought I might be sick. Because I knew with brutal, terrifying clarity what Nathan had done.

Lyra told us how the dagger worked. Bonds. Blood. "You forced a mating bond." I hadn't meant to say the words out loud, but they feathered past my lips. Nathan's mouth curled into a cruel smile, and my stomach lurched.

The memories I'd tried so hard to lock away came crashing back, playing out in vivid flashes. Nathan looming over me, his expression twisted with lust and rage. His hands brutal and punishing on my skin. The overwhelming pain and helplessness as he took what he wanted over and over again. The sheer terror when I'd tried to leave the first time, and he'd caught me with my bag at the back door.

A wounded sound worked its way out of my throat. My knees buckled, and I sank to the ground, fighting to breathe past the panic clawing at my chest. Why did he still have a hold on me?

Dimly, I registered Rowan's answering roar of anguish and outrage. I'd never heard anything so primal, so agonized. In my peripheral vision, I saw his body shaking violently, saw the wolf within him begging to be unleashed.

But he didn't shift. With what looked like gargantuan effort, Rowan held his beast back and launched himself at

Nathan in his human form. The two alphas collided with a sickening crunch.

Why wasn't he shifting? Rowan had felt Nathan's power just as I had, and he'd be stronger, faster as a wolf. Then again...so would Nathan.

"Rowan!" Finally, I forced his name out, but it was too late. Fabric ripped, bones cracked, and feral snarls rent the air. The sounds of a brutal, no-holds-barred fight to the death. That's what this was. That's what Nathan had wanted. I was sure of it.

"You'll stay there like a good bitch," Nathan growled, and his authority clammed my hands and knees to the ground. I couldn't move. Couldn't force more than my head up from the ground.

And all I could do was stare at Callista's limp form, my heart fracturing into countless razor-sharp shards. I'd failed her. Now I'd failed Rowan and his pack.

How many more people would become casualties of Nathan's obsession with me?

I gasped as Rowan managed to slam his fist into Nathan's face with a sickening crunch. Blood spurted from the other alpha's nose as his head snapped back.

But he recovered with preternatural speed, lips curling in a taunting smile even as crimson streamed down his face. "Feisty. But I don't know if she's worth all this." Nathan laughed, the sound as cold and sharp as the damn dagger. "Trust me. I speak from experience."

Nathan's retaliating blow shattered Rowan's kneecap. My heart seized as Rowan's leg buckled, and he barely caught himself before crumpling. A ragged cry tore from his throat, agony etched into every line of his face.

Still, he didn't shift. *Why the hell wasn't he shifting?* Desperation pumped through my veins as I watched the man I loved absorbing hit after devastating hit. *I loved him.* The realization hit as powerfully as the fear and disgust had slammed into me seconds before. He was nothing like Nathan Black—nothing like the alpha I thought him to be. He carried his strength and authority, never using it for his own gain. He was loyal. Kind. And he was fighting *for me.*

But Nathan held the dagger. He'd perverted the ways of the pack to gain the dark power that oozed from him like rot. Now Nathan was toying with him, a predator playing with its prey. Enjoying Rowan's pain and despair. Each carefully targeted strike left Rowan more broken, more debilitated.

I screamed for Rowan's pack, my voice snapping against the trees. *Why weren't they stepping in?* Tears streamed down my cheeks as I clawed my fingers into the dirt. "Stop! Nathan, stop!"

Even with our healing abilities, I'd never seen anyone withstand such catastrophic damage and remain standing. Rowan's body was a map of brutality—skin shredded, bones snapped, blood flowing in scarlet rivers.

But his eyes, those piercing blue eyes that had first captivated me, remained locked on Nathan. Blazing with unbreakable determination even as the light in them dimmed with each passing second.

I wrapped my arms around myself, trying to hold the broken pieces together. But it was too much. Too much...

I wanted to shift. To fight. But Nathan's power held me rooted to the spot. "Rowan," I whispered brokenly, my wolf howling in anguish deep inside me. I couldn't lose him. Not like this. Not when we'd only just found each other.

As if he'd heard my silent plea, Rowan met my gaze across the blood-soaked ground. In that infinite moment, a thousand unspoken words passed between us.

"I always loved it when you begged, Evs." Nathan watched

my face as he wrapped a hand around Rowan's throat and squeezed.

TWENTY-NINE

ROWAN

The world around me blurred as I fought to stay upright. Pain radiated from my shattered knee, every step, agony. Wolves healed fast, but not that fast. I immediately searched for Evelyn, her face twisted and streaked with tears as Jasper held her with Blake standing close by.

Good. I hated that I couldn't be the one to comfort her, but was grateful that he'd heard my call to go to her. Nathan's power wouldn't let her rise, and if she tried, she'd only tear herself apart.

I needed to focus, which was damn near impossible with Evelyn breaking and my body right there along with her. I hadn't meant to wait as long as I did, but Nathan's power was staggering. It hurt my pride to admit it, but it was true. I'd realized the drawbacks of my plan the second I'd rushed into the clearing.

I needed hands to hold that canister, which meant I couldn't shift. It was a risk, and I wasn't sure yet if it had paid off.

I finally had him where I wanted him. My shoulder strained as I reached into the waistband of my jeans, pulling the canister free. Finn had said it wouldn't take much to activate, and I was counting on it.

With a guttural yell, I swung my arm up, slamming the metal into Nathan's jaw. A low hiss sounded, and I forced my arm to stay put. I had no proof that whatever Lyra had given me wouldn't affect me, too. But I had faith.

She was a witch, and she'd given it to me for a reason.

Nathan's hand flinched, giving me enough space to tear myself away from him and drag in a much-needed breath. Nathan staggered back.

I had to take advantage. I hadn't been able to shift before, but there was nothing holding me back now. I finally let my wolf forward, gritting my teeth against the pain as I shifted through my broken bones.

Nathan was in front of me, gasping for air, but it only took him a split second to follow suit. If he'd been smart, he would've shifted a long time ago. I would've had to hail Mary the concoction from Lyra and Finn. But I'd counted on his arrogance—his desire to prove he was stronger when we had equal footing.

Or maybe he'd just wanted to hold that damn dagger.

I stumbled and caught my body with my forearms just as Nathan leaped. Evelyn's voice broke through my haze. "He's dying, Jasper! He's my mate!"

Jasper's voice was gruff, pulling her back. "You have to trust him."

I gritted my teeth and forced myself to stand. I had to finish this. It wouldn't be enough to incapacitate Nathan, not with as far as he'd gone and the power he'd acquired through the dagger. He had to die. And it had to be me who took his last breath.

Nathan's dominance wavered, his movements faltering. It was now or never. I pushed off the ground, muscles coiled and ready. Despite the searing pain, I forced myself to move, to fight. Nathan lashed out with teeth bared, but I ducked and countered with a swift kick to his ribs.

He swung again, slower, and I seized the opportunity to drive my shoulder into his jaw. Nathan staggered, but he wasn't done. He lunged at me, claws extended, and I barely dodged in time, his claws grazing my side.

Then he was on me, his wolf tearing into the flesh of my shoulder. I whirled, trying to shake him free, but he was rabid. Feral. I stumbled at the pain, the loss of blood. Nathan dragged me to my side, my fur matted and bloodied. I dug for anything —scraping for any last scrap of energy to fight.

"Don't you dare leave me!" Evelyn screamed, and suddenly, the bond between us yawned wide open. The vision of Nathan's wolf above me transformed back into the man, his face red and twisted with rage.

"You act like you have any better options. Who wouldn't want to be claimed by the alpha of Kitimat? What I'm giving you right now is a gift, Evelyn. You should try and be more grateful."

The image was so crisp, so realistic, I knew exactly where it came from. Evelyn. He'd said that to Evelyn. He'd put his hands on *my mate*. A rage so deep and hot bubbled in my core until it expanded and exploded outward.

I ripped myself free, leaving flesh and fur in his jaws, then charged his back legs, feeling the satisfying crunch of bone against my skull.

Nathan roared, swinging wildly, but his strikes lost their precision. For the first time, fear flickered in his eyes.

Good, asshole. You should be afraid.

I ducked under another swipe and slammed my paw into his stomach. As he tried to recover, I drove for his jugular. Pain shot through my leg with every move, but I wouldn't stop. He would pay for what he'd done to Evelyn and the she-wolf lying on the grass ahead of us. No other woman would have to fear because of his power. Because of his abuse.

Nathan wriggled free and reeled on me, his golden eyes wild and desperate. I used his momentum against him, flipping him over my shoulder and slamming him into the ground. He groaned, working to get up, but I was already on him, my teeth sinking deep into his throat.

Blood sprayed, and my own strength began to wane. My knee screamed in protest, but I had to finish this. Nathan struggled, and I locked my jaw, crushing his windpipe. He choked, but I didn't let up. I shook my head fiercely, tearing into his flesh, showing no mercy.

It was justice.

It was the way of the pack.

"Rowan." Mara's voice sounded behind me, and I realized Nathan's body had gone limp, the light in his eyes extinguished.

I released him, panting heavily, and looked up at the moon. My wolf howled, long and slow. The grief, exhaustion, and victory blurring into one emotion that humans didn't have words for.

Evelyn's howl joined mine, a haunting sound of triumph and mourning. I turned to her, my chest heaving, and saw relief in the eyes of her trembling wolf.

Strawberry. After hearing Nathan call her Evs, I would never, ever let that syllable leave my lips again. I tried to stand, to limp over to her, but could barely summon the strength to whine.

She dropped to the ground, nuzzling against me as the rest of my pack rushed to release the wolves still in duress.

Report, I pushed through the pack bond.

Clear. Tori responded immediately.

I turned my head. Where the hell was Jasper?

Releasing the last she-wolf now, Lana cut in.

Jasper, I growled. Panic edged up my throat. He'd been with Blake. What if—

You're not going to like this. Jasper pushed through finally, his communication rough and winded. *That scent Evelyn found? Ash and I caught a whiff of it. Right after I noticed the dagger was gone.*

CHAPTER

THIRTY

The remnants of my wolf's fury simmered beneath my skin, a primal surge of alpha power coursing through my veins. I drew a deep breath, inhaling the crisp night air, allowing the earth beneath my paws and the breeze through my fur to ground me.

Evelyn was safe. My pack was safe. That fact whispered through my mind like a balm, soothing the raw edges of my instincts. I wasn't ignoring the fact that we'd lost the dagger, but that problem would have to wait for another day.

Beneath the sharp scent of pine was the tang of blood—my blood. I dropped to my knees, and my wolf fell back, leaving me shivering and naked in the clover.

"Rowan!" Evelyn's voice, laced with urgency and relief, cut through the haze in my head. I felt her before I saw her. She was human again. Wearing loose pants and a T-shirt.

186

Evelyn dropped to the ground next to me, her arms wrapping around my neck, her lips finding mine in a series of frantic kisses. I groaned, and she pulled away just enough to look into my eyes. The moonlight illuminated the gold flecks in her irises, shimmering with unshed tears.

"Stay still." Her hands were gentle as they roamed over me, assessing the damage. The rest of the pack circled around us, their faces etched with concern and awe. A woman was slumped between Lana and Tori.

"She's unharmed?" I worked to keep my eyes open.

"Shh." Evelyn ran a hand over my cheek. My pack had seen me fight, seen me protect what was ours, but now they watched as my mate took charge of my care.

"Get me some water, bandages, and clean cloths!" Evelyn snapped, her med kit already open and her skilled hands working methodically. The pack moved to obey, their swift actions a testament to their respect for her.

"I'm fine," I murmured, trying to ease the worry creasing her brow. "I heal fast."

"Fast isn't good enough," she retorted, her fingers deft as she cleaned a gash on my shoulder. "What the hell were you thinking? You could've told me what you were planning. I could've—"

I shook my head. "It had to be me."

She shot me a look. Her rebuke warmed me more than it chided. Evelyn's fierceness, her strength and independence, were some of the many qualities I loved about her. Even if the combination annoyed the hell out of me.

With each careful touch, I felt the bond between us pulse. She was safe. She had no reason to run from Kitimat or Black Lake.

Whispers from my pack rustled like leaves, but I couldn't make them out. My senses were dull, my head foggy. I grimaced as Evelyn forced my leg into a new, straighter position.

A sudden hush fell over the clearing as two figures emerged from the shadows. Tori and Jasper approached, their expressions grim, and I could sense the shift in the mood of my pack.

Tori stepped forward, her eyes locked onto mine. "There's a trail leading away from here, but it's nearly impossible to track."

Jasper looked grim.

"I sensed it," Evelyn murmured, her hand pausing on my skin. "I still don't know what it means."

Questions swirled in my head, a tempest threatening to roar to life. Nathan's defeat should have been the end of it, but the missing dagger suggested otherwise. Who was behind his actions? What was the true nature of the threat we faced?

Gathering my strength, I pushed myself to sit, nodding at Evelyn as she reluctantly moved back. I wished I had a plan, some wise advice. The truth was, my pack was on edge. I could sense it through the bond, and I was barely able to stay upright.

I looked up at the moon, wondering if the rest of our pack had followed the elders and done a full moon run without me. I doubted it.

I wanted to know what the truth was about the ritual we'd witnessed and the missing relic. But we needed to bond together, not split up again on patrols.

"We all want answers," I started. "We will get them. But right now, we need rest. Go home to your families. Check on your pack mates. We'll reconvene in—"

"Rowan," Tori interjected. "You can't ignore the fact that the Kitimat are without a leader now." She took a step forward, her eyes holding mine. "You defeated their alpha. You need to take charge. Unite both packs under your leadership. It's the only way to ensure stability and safety for all."

Her words sank into me like water on soil. She was right—I knew it. But would Kitimat accept it? Would they unite under the pack they'd been taught to despise since birth? Would Black Lake accept them?

We had Nathan's second restrained back at Tori's. The last thing I wanted to do was talk to that asshole. But if I couldn't force his loyalty, what hope did I have for the rest of the pack?

Unity. It was a hope. One I had to keep alive.

But if I'd learned anything as alpha over the past few years it was that respect and trust had to be earned. If Blake, Nathan's third had defected, how much proof would Kitimat need to believe their alpha wasn't worth following?

Strength didn't equal an iron paw.

It was up to me to show them something different.

CHAPTER

THIRTY-ONE

The door to Rowan's house swung open with a whisper of sound, and I stepped through the threshold. My legs felt like they were encased in concrete.

"Rowan," I murmured, half-supporting the weight of his solid frame as we shuffled toward the sanctuary of his bedroom. His breaths were labored, a sign of his still-mending body, and yet, there was strength in his grip around my shoulders. Strength that spoke of an alpha who would bend but never break.

"Easy," I whispered, guiding him down to the bed. His blue eyes met mine, a silent thank you passing between us as I gently removed the boots Jasper had lent him, setting them against the wall.

My mate. The words pulsed with the beat of my heart. As I'd watched him fight with my palms forced to the dirt, I'd known the truth with every cell in my body. There was nothing else for me. I couldn't imagine my life without Rowan Steele, and I'd almost had to watch him be stripped from me.

"Rest." My voice caught, and Rowan's gaze sharpened.

"Evelyn—"

"Later. I promise." I leaned over him, pressing my lips to his forehead. Rowan sank into the mattress.

I watched his eyelids shutter closed. This formidable alpha of the Black Lake Pack laid bare and vulnerable beneath me. His dark hair on the pillow. His lashes brushing his cheeks.

I settled myself into the chair beside his bed, watching over him as the moon rose high outside the window. There was nowhere else I'd rather be. As my breathing deepened, I clung to the stirrings of a bond that ran deeper than blood—a connection I planned to etch into my soul.

THE DOOR CREAKED, and my eyes shot open, my wolf jumping to the surface. I jumped from my chair and shot into the hall, then froze. Two of Rowan's pack mates stepped inside, their arms heavy with bowls and a casserole dish. The scent of roasted meat and freshly baked bread made my mouth water.

"Morning, Evelyn," the woman with her hair pulled back into a braid gave a quick smile before heading to the kitchen.

I didn't know either of them, but that didn't matter. They were my pack now. My throat tightened at the realization that they'd accepted me—a Kitimat, a defector—long before I'd accepted them.

"Thank you," I murmured as they set the feast down on the counter, steam curling in the air.

"Make sure he eats. You, too." The man put his hand on my shoulder.

"Get your damn hands off my mate, Andrew!" Rowan barked from the bedroom.

A smile split Andrew's face. "There he is." He made his way back to the door, and I could barely wait for them to walk out the door before rushing back to the bedroom.

"You're up. Can I get you—"

"I want you." Rowan held out his hand.

I took it but didn't allow him to pull me to the bed. "You need to eat something."

"That was my plan." He gave a wicked grin, and my cheeks heated.

"Nice try." I raised an eyebrow. "You might not be willing to admit weakness, but I'm not going to let you ignore your body's needs."

"Not all needs are created equal."

I laughed as he yanked on my wrist, and I dropped onto the bed next to him. Rowan's hands were instantly on my skin, slipping up the back of my shirt. I dropped my head and pressed my lips to his.

"How about we go in order," I whispered.

"Your way or my way?"

I grinned against his mouth. "Mine."

"Which is?"

"Food. Then a shower."

With a slow nod, he pushed himself up into a sitting position, leaning back against the headboard. "Only if you join me."

"Deal." It was the simplest agreement I'd made in weeks. I made up our plates, and we sat together, sighing with the pleasure of filling our bellies with roast beef, glazed carrots, and fresh rolls.

After a few mouthfuls, I dipped a cloth into the bowl of cool water I'd fetched earlier, wringing it out before placing it gently on his forehead. His eyes closed at the touch, a sigh escaping his lips.

"Thank you," he murmured, his hand reaching up to cover mine where it rested on the cloth, his grip firm but tender. "For everything."

Sunlight played across Rowan's features, softening the hard angles of his jaw and igniting the streaks of pale blue in his eyes. His dark hair was tousled, and I ran a hand through it.

"Did you sleep at all?" Concern knitted his brow.

"Enough," I lied, brushing off the question with a small smile. My gaze lingered on his face, on the faint shadow of stubble and the fullness of his lips.

Rowan wrapped a hand around my neck, his touch sending a jolt of electricity through me. I hastily stacked our plates and set them on the nightstand.

The intensity of his gaze held me captive, and I couldn't resist leaning in, drawn by a force stronger than my own will. Our lips met, and his scent, the taste of him—wild and familiar —ignited a spark that flared into a flame.

Rowan's hand cradled my cheek, angling my head as the kiss deepened. The world narrowed to the space between us, where every brush of skin lit me up like a flare. Desire curled in my belly. It was a need that went beyond the physical, echoing the call of our inner wolves, the primal part of our nature that recognized its mate.

We were both starved for this connection and now that I knew, nothing was holding us back.

Rowan pulled back, his eyes searching mine.

"Yes," I answered before he could ask the question. "I'm yours, Rowan."

"Your life in Seattle—"

"I don't give a shit about Seattle."

Rowan's grip tightened on my neck. "What about Bruce?"

I laughed out loud, collapsing onto his chest. "I mentioned him one time. How the hell do you remember his name?"

"You were talking to another man on the phone. He's on my kill list."

I tipped my head and playfully nipped his jaw with my teeth.

"Don't tease unless you're ready to pay the price." Rowan threw me over onto my back, covering me with his body. The weight of him pressed me into the mattress, stealing the breath from my lungs.

He pressed his knee between my legs, and I arched into him. "We haven't showered."

"You win some, you lose some." Rowan's lips were on my skin, his hands frantically pulling at my shirt.

I grabbed at his gray t-shirt. "I thought you said we were going to take our time."

"That was before I had to wait a damn week." With a growl of frustration, Rowan ripped my shirt open, pulling the torn fabric off my midsection. His eyes darkened, his breath coming in short bursts.

"I never sleep in a bra," I whispered.

The sheets caressed my skin as Rowan shuddered and pulled me further down the bed toward him.

"What thread count are these?"

"You're asking about my sheets right now?" Rowan traced the lines and curves of my body with his fingers, his eyes hungry.

"They're soft. I like them."

"I like you in them." He lowered his head to my stomach, his lips grazing my skin, and my fingers tangled in his dark hair, pulling him closer, needing to feel every inch of him.

Rowan growled low in his throat, the sound igniting a primal fire deep within me. His strong hands roamed my curves. "My mate," Rowan's hands tightened on my hips. "My heart. My everything."

He nipped at the bone of my hip, making me gasp. "Tell me what you want." His voice was raw, pleading.

I looped my calves over his ankles. "Make me yours. Please."

He lifted his cheek from my stomach, and his lips crashed against mine, his tongue slipping into my mouth. I gripped his neck and poured all my longing into the kiss, feeling the desperation radiating off him in electric pulses. Every brush of our tongues, every shared breath, deepened our connection until I felt both hollowed out and full to bursting.

"You're everything," he gasped, his hands roaming over my body, reading me like braille. "I've waited for this. I've waited for you."

I didn't know it, but I'd been waiting for him, too. My existence in Seattle was pond water. Stagnant. Starting to stink. But before I saw Rowan again, I didn't think I had another option. Now, I felt connected with a crystal clear mountain stream. Fresh and life-giving.

"Damn, Strawberry," he murmured, his voice thick with longing.

The scent of our desire hung heavy in the air, a heady mix that filled my senses and set my blood aflame. We undressed each other slowly, deliberately, savoring that moment as though it were the last. My heart raced as his fingers brushed against my spine, sending waves of heat cascading through me.

"Rowan." His name scraped from me like a plea. An invitation. I leaned closer, feeling the warmth radiate from him. His fingertips danced along my collarbone, igniting sparks of desire that plummeted to my hips.

My wolf thrummed beneath my skin, yearning to connect

with her mate. She paced restlessly, whining with need, desperate to complete our bond. It was a primal, spiritual longing that transcended the physical.

As Rowan pressed hard against me, I sensed the same desperation in him. His wolf called to mine, their spirits begging to intertwine.

"I can feel it," I whispered. "Our wolves, our souls...they're meant to be one."

Rowan's eyes shone with fierce love as he settled between my thighs. "You're my soulmate, my other half. Without you, I'm incomplete."

Tears pricked my eyes at his words, the depth of our connection overwhelming me. I pulled him closer, wanting to be filled, to be consumed by him. With a surge of urgency, our bodies moved as one, pressed so tight that our edges blurred together.

In that sacred moment, we were no longer two separate beings but one soul sharing two bodies. I clung to him, my nails digging into his back as my mouth filled with heat. My fangs lowered as pleasure coursed through me, my heart desperately trying to keep up.

"Mark me," I gasped, my body so tight and hot, it didn't feel like my own.

His eyes darkened with intent as I bared my neck for him, and he sank his teeth into my flesh, a sharp bite that sent a wave of ecstasy surging through my veins.

"Rowan—" I was going to shatter. I was—

Rowan gasped, his eyes nearly black as he wrapped his hands over the crown of my head and rocked into me. My fangs retracted, and I wrapped my legs around his hips, crying out.

My hands—my claws—

His blood was hot and wet on my fingertips. *I had marked*

him. My wolf was satisfied, and the world around us faded, dissolving into an ethereal haze.

"Together," Rowan gasped, our bodies wild and furious, his alpha energy washing through me like a drug.

"Yes," I moaned, our connection swelling like a rising tide, pulling us closer to the brink, crashing against the cliffs. I couldn't think except in colors. "Rowan!" My voice was swallowed in his flesh as I pressed into his shoulder, my teeth scraping against his skin, begging for release.

"You. Are. *Mine.*"

Lights exploded behind my eyes as we crested the peak, our bodies trembling as if caught in a tempest. Rowan's body bucked, both of us gasping for breath as my arms crossed over his slick skin, completely useless.

I seemed to float, weightless and free, my cheek pressed against Rowan's flushed neck as his arms gave way. He collapsed against me, his heart gradually beginning to slow against my chest.

I threaded my fingers in the damp hair against the base of his neck. *Mine.* Rowan Steele was mine.

My wolf howled her approval as we lay there, basking in the afterglow, our bodies intertwined, our souls forever bound by our love and the mated bond of our wolves.

"Did you have any idea?" I whispered, my voice raw.

"Hell no. Or I wouldn't have waited."

I laughed as Rowan's lips grazed my temple. "Do you think it will be that way every time?"

He grinned against my skin. "Damn straight."

CHAPTER
THIRTY-TWO

I opened my eyes to the room bathed in a soft golden glow. Sunlight filtered through the cracks in the curtains, casting dappled patterns on the walls. The bedding beneath us was in disarray, a testament to the thirty-six hours we'd spent there.

The shower was running. For the seventh time.

I grinned, stretching my arms behind my head. I could still feel Evelyn's body imprinted on my skin, the heat of her searing into my bones.

This was what it felt like to claim and be claimed. To entrust the key to your heart to another and hope they didn't break it.

You gonna step out into the sunlight anytime soon, bud? Jasper's voice hummed in my head.

Green isn't a good color on you, I sent back, then followed up with, *Weren't you the one who said I needed to take this mating thing more seriously?*

I regret everything.

I chuckled, tossing off the sheets. *I'll meet you at the garage.*

As much as I didn't want to leave Evelyn's side, I needed to talk with Jasper and Lana. I needed to meet with Blake and have a heart-to-heart with Justin before approaching Kitimat. Some of their pack members had already come sniffing around. I needed to nail down a plan for integration.

We would be one pack again.

The thought made my throat tighten. It wouldn't be as simple as that, and I wasn't naive enough to believe it would be. Nathan had challenged my father, and we were still knee-deep in the fallout.

But I'd learned from that experience. I knew we could do it differently.

I entered the bathroom and opened the glass door, stepping in beside Evelyn. Eyes heavy with contentment, she turned to face me as my hand skimmed along the soft curve of her hips.

"Morning." I breathed her in, and a shiver ran through me when I caught my scent still on her skin. I wanted her to get out of the damn shower so every wolf in my pack would know I'd left my mark.

"Morning." Her cheeks flushed under my scrutiny.

I couldn't help but smile, the memory of the night before flooding back to me in vivid detail. The hunger in her eyes, the way she'd let me devour her and begged for more.

I pulled her into my arms, the water cascading over our skin. "I have to go to work."

"You mean we can't hole up here forever?" She tipped her head, grinning up at me. I ran my fingers over the mark I'd left on her neck, already healed into a dark whorl that looked curiously like a berry on the end of a stem.

"Have you seen yours yet?" she asked, turning me around and running her fingers over my skin.

"Describe it."

"*Them*." Her touch sent prickles over my skin. "There are three over your shoulder blade. They look almost like cedars."

That was perfect. The trees were my refuge, and that's what I wanted to be for my mate. My pack. I turned back to face her. "You drew blood."

Evelyn rolled her eyes. "And you didn't?"

I grinned, dropping my head until my lips met hers. "I love you."

She pulled against my hips. "I love you, too." Without warning, she smacked her hand against my bare ass. "Now stop stealing all my water."

CHAPTER

THIRTY-THREE

Evelyn

The house was too still. I paced the length of our living room, my feet sinking into the plush carpet, the silence punctuated by the rhythmic tap of my nails against my jeans. Each tick of the clock heightened my nerves.

"Come on, Lana." I raked a hand through my auburn hair. Rowan had said she'd be back by dusk, and the sun was already dipping behind the trees.

Nothing could've gone wrong, right? She was only clearing out my things, and it wasn't like I had much. I both hated and loved that Rowan wouldn't let me go with her. I understood him wanting to keep me safe, but to make Lana do my apartment cleaning and check out? That didn't seem fair.

I paused by the window and pressed my forehead against the cool glass. Finally, a gravelly rumble broke the silence as an

201

SUV pulling a U-Haul trailer rolled up the drive, dust swirling in its wake. My pulse quickened, and I swung the door open before the engine cut out, the crisp evening air a slap against my flushed skin.

"Hey!" Lana dropped from the vehicle, her dark hair cascading around her shoulders, looking every bit the badass third-in-command she was. My anxiety melted away as she wrapped her strong arms around me.

"Did you miss me that much?" Lana teased, pulling back to look at me with a smirk. Her gaze was assessing, but the edge of concern there told me she understood the gravity of what today meant for both of us.

"Don't flatter yourself." I grinned, and it felt good to smile, to let Lana's easy confidence buffer the storm of emotions inside me.

"Good answer, Beta." Lana nudged me with her shoulder, her eyes sparkling. "You ready for the pack meeting tomorrow?"

"Ready as I'll ever be." Which was...not ready at all. The weight of the upcoming gathering settled over me. It wasn't just any meeting—it was my first step into this new life. The moment I took my place in Black Lake as Rowan's other half.

"Let's get your stuff inside." Lana gestured to the bags and boxes in the back of the SUV. "The boys will be over in a sec to unload the trailer. Then we can plot how to survive the pack's curiosity about their alpha's new mate."

Interest was a mild way to put it. Rowan Steele had staked his claim, and while his friends were quick to accept me, I wasn't so sure about the elders. Or the members of what used to be Kitimat.

"Don't think about it too hard." Lana pulled the door open. "You haven't talked to your parents in years, right? So no difference if they don't accept you now."

How had she known what I was thinking? "I feel like there is a difference."

Lana nudged my elbow as she walked by with a box. "We're your family now, Evelyn. You're not getting rid of us."

Twenty minutes later, boxes and bags littered the living room floor, a tangible mosaic of my fractured life. My fingers traced over a leather-bound album peeking out from a box, its corners worn.

Callie walked through the door, and I leaped up from the floor. "What are you doing here?"

"I heard it was moving day."

I ran to her and wrapped her in a hug. "You look good."

"Slightly better than last week?"

I laughed, though it was hardly a funny statement. We still had so much to talk about. I hoped she'd open up to me, but there were things I needed to tell her first. Though I'd let her keep my number when I left, I'd never opened up about what had happened behind Nathan's closed door. My stomach ached at the thought that now when I told her, she'd understand fully.

I pulled back, and the soft buzz of my phone against the table cut through our greeting. I walked back and picked it up.

BRUCE:

> Training newbies is a nightmare. Where'd you stash the bandage scissors?

I couldn't suppress the smirk that danced on my lips.

> Probably the same place you left your manscaper

Bruce:

So…your sister's room?

I snorted, then turned the screen to Callista.

"Aww. He misses you."

I'd told Callista about my coworkers months ago. I never imagined I'd be standing next to her in person texting one of them back in Seattle.

BRUCE:

Probably good you went back to Canada. This election's going to be a shit show

Take care, Jack

I turned off the screen and set it back on the table.

Callista sighed. "You'll miss this chaos?"

"Maybe just a little," I admitted to myself, a pang of fondness for the controlled pandemonium of the ER piercing through me. It was where I thrived, where every day was high-stakes. Though being here wasn't much different.

"When do you start with the EMTs here in Black Lake?" Lana asked, directing Liam to the kitchen with a box of my pots and pans.

"Next week."

"Good. They could use someone like you." Her approval warmed me more than I expected.

"Thanks, Lana." I smiled, genuinely touched by her endorsement. But then, my attention snagged on someone else entirely.

Rowan.

He strode through the threshold, his arms laden with the

last of my belongings, muscles flexing under the strain. There was a primal satisfaction in watching him, an alpha claiming space for his mate within his territory. My heart raced at the sight, my wolf stirring at the scent of him.

Lana smirked. "Looks like the alpha has everything under control."

"Always does," I murmured, unable to tear my eyes away.

The rest of the pack cleared out, inviting Callista along to the pub. For a split second, I considered going with them. Grabbing on to Rowan and pulling him out for a drink, possibly another game of pool with lower stakes.

But I knew we had things to discuss for the meeting.

Lana grabbed her leather jacket off the back of a chair and made for the door. "See you at the gathering."

"See you there," I called, watching as the door closed behind her.

No sooner had Lana left than Rowan emerged from the bedroom, a misplaced box of my belongings in his arms. He set it in the living room by the others, his back muscles shifting beneath his shirt as he straightened up.

"Satisfied?" I grinned as he strode toward me.

"Very." He circled his arms around me and pulled me close. "Are you upset you didn't get to go back? Get closure?"

I shook my head. "Lana's the one who had to clean my stove."

He kissed the bridge of my nose. "I hope it was a disaster."

I laughed, pushing away to start unpacking.

"Leave it," he murmured against my ear, his breath sending shivers down my spine.

"But—" I started to protest, though the heat of his body was quickly melting any resolve I had.

"Later." His hands were gentle yet insistent as they guided

me away from the mess. "Right now, you're where you need to be."

Before I could respond, he scooped me up effortlessly, my world narrowing to the blue of his eyes and the strength of his embrace. There was no space for words as he carried me into the bedroom, the door closing behind us.

EPILOGUE

CALLISTA

My smile faded as I stepped out into the crisp afternoon air, my boots crunching against the gravel. I made my way to where my Jeep waited patiently, and as I reached the door and inserted the key, a sudden wave of exhaustion crashed over me. It was as if every ounce of energy had been siphoned from my body in an instant. The joy from moments before evaporated, replaced by a bone-deep fatigue that made my shoulders slump forward involuntarily.

"Keep it together," I muttered to myself, fighting against the invisible weight pressing down on me. The sunlight seemed dimmer now, the shadows stretching long and ominous across the empty street. My movements grew sluggish, each action requiring monumental effort as though I were wading through mud.

I rolled up my sleeve and inspected the cut along my forearm. It still hadn't healed. *Why the hell hadn't it healed?*

I dropped my head on the steering wheel, memories of Nathan binding my wrists. Of forcing the dagger against my skin.

That was why I'd stolen it. After that night, when he'd coerced me into his home, I knew I couldn't leave it in his possession. But now? I wondered if that was what he'd wanted all along.

Not him, I reminded myself. The darkness.

That was what I called him. The being I'd sensed in the shadows. The one I knew had been watching in the woods when Rowan defeated Nathan. The one who still had the precious relic.

I could feel its dark whispers at the edge of my consciousness, a haunting melody that promised power but threatened to consume me whole.

I gripped the wheel, taking in slow, measured breaths, then forced myself to confront the mundane reality of my Jeep's interior. I didn't want to leave, but the conflicting desires churned like a tempest inside me. The dagger's dark allure was intoxicating.

You know where it is.

My wolf whined, curling up and burying her head.

The scent hit me then, sudden and intrusive. It wound its way through the slightly ajar window, bypassing the mundane odors of pine and asphalt. My nostrils flared involuntarily, the wolf within roused by the unfamiliar trace lingering on the breeze. It was subtle but distinct.

I shouldn't follow. I should start the Jeep and drive away from this place, from the siren call that beckoned me into the wilds. But the fragrance stirred something primal within me, a yearning that was not entirely my own.

The cut on my arm burned.

I pressed the start button, and the engine roared to life beneath me. The road ahead blurred as I drove.

I was going home to Blake and Celeste. I was going to the pack meeting tomorrow. I was going to work with Blake, Rowan, and Evelyn to blend Black Lake with Kitimat. I was...

I blinked, the road suddenly looking less familiar. Had I turned? I glanced back but couldn't see a road that I'd missed.

An ominous chill crept over my skin as dusk cloaked the world in shades of gray. My grip on the steering wheel tightened, knuckles straining against the leather.

Come to me, Callista.

I'm waiting.

ABOUT THE AUTHOR

 Luna masquerades as a well-adjusted, functioning adult, but she secretly still believes in magic and wild things hidden just beyond the veil of our world. She has a fairy garden (with lights!) and lives with her husband and children near the Rocky Mountains in Colorado. She adores shiny objects.